You Should Probably Leave

Avery Queen

This is a work of fiction. Names, characters, organizations, places, events, and incidents are either the product of imagination by the author or are used fictitiously. Any resemblance to actual persons, living or dead, or actual events is entirely coincidental.

ISBN: 9798989316922

Editing by Whitney Morsillo of Whitney's Book Works

Cover Design by Pretty Indie Book Cover Design

This book is dedicated to my husband. When he finally decides to read one of my books then he will know just how much I love him and I even dedicated a whole page to him. Thanks for letting me write whenever I felt the need to. Love you, babe.

Chapter 1
The Past is Forever

He pushed me up against the wall, letting my ex's oversized painting that I hated from day one, drop to the ground as his fingers reached my jeans, ripping the button open and aggressively reaching to the base of my thong. He pulled it aside and rubbed his fingers along my pleasure pebble and then toward my lips, splitting them and entering me fast and hard. My jeans were getting in the way of letting me reach the climax that I needed. I quickly stopped him and pushed him off me, slipping my jeans off and tossing them aside.

He returned against my body, groaning as his dick rubbed hard against my stomach through his jeans. He would be deeper inside me in a minute, in my stomach, and for that, I was excited. I needed a release, and he was going to be it. He looked down at me, lifting my face up toward him with the fingers he just had inside me, forcing them onto my tongue and making me suck them dry. I never knew I wanted a taste until he did that. A sex craze came over me, and I wanted more. I took his fingers and pushed them back inside me, letting me reach another orgasm, my face flushing with heat. I grabbed his fingers and brought them back to my mouth while my free hand rubbed on his dick. He groaned and dropped his jeans, then returned my hand to his shaft. The veins started to pump harder. He could no longer take the wait. I grinned when I knew he had reached his limit of teasing and foreplay.

He lifted me up against the wall and entered me raw. My fingered wet pussy let him slide into me, reaching the length of me. He pulled out and pushed in harder, making my entire body tremble against the wall, but somehow, he knew it was exactly what I wanted. He slowly pulled back out and then slammed into me again. Each time getting deeper, making my pussy stretch to his length. I wanted him to reach the middle of my stomach, and now.

"Harder," I whispered, between panting breaths.

He obeyed and didn't hesitate, forcing the rest of the pictures on the wall to fall off, shattering as he continued. Each thrust harder than the last, making me reach the edge. I grabbed the back of his head for leverage that I truly didn't need, wanting every inch of him to be closer as I let my head lean up toward the ceiling and take it all in. His lips met my neck as he sucked hard, leaving a hickey that would be hard to cover up in the morning, before wandering down to my nipples, tugging at them with his teeth, but the sensation made me ready to climax. He knew what he was doing. He knew how to make me finish. Didn't matter how many years had passed between us. He knew I would always willingly be his late night fuck.

Feeling his dick move inside me, letting me push back against him, was almost too much. He began to reach his end as his panting sped up, and the sweat between us started to drip. We were going to cum together in five, four, three, two, one… release.

He let himself linger at the edge of my cervix, pushing deeper into me. The need was there for both of us, or maybe it was the tequila. Could never go wrong with shots of pure liquid courage after a long day of bullshit. I could still taste the lime on my lips, or maybe it was from his. Our breathing was heavy after the release of what we both needed. *A goodbye fuck*. But we both knew that we could never truly say goodbye. We had too much history that was sure to reveal itself at some point. It was only a matter of time before the flooding of emotions broke through the already too high gates that were trying to keep me safe from feeling. The fucking universe always had a way of pushing us back together, even when I least expected it. And bonus, his dick felt so good that it was always hard to say no to him. No one had ever been able to get me this wet before. If he wasn't such an asshole, then maybe we could stay together. Though in reality, he wasn't an asshole at all. I was. I couldn't settle down yet, and I couldn't face the past just yet, either. My mind raced. I needed to stop overthinking.

His dick started to pump inside me again, bringing me back to the now. I needed this distraction. I could feel him getting hard again. Was he ready for another go? *I fucking hope so.* My overthinking was not going to let me sleep tonight. I wanted to keep cumming until the sun came up. He lifted me off the wall and walked me to the kitchen, laying me on the small table. I pushed the place settings off that my mother had bought me for Thanksgiving. I didn't give a shit. I never had people over here for gatherings. I didn't need them. I didn't need anything or anyone. But I sure as hell was thankful for this giving. I needed this. I needed him to stay tonight. I knew I would regret it in the morning, but right now, being alone didn't seem like a good option with the hangover that was sure to come in the morning.

He thrusted harder against me, pushing deeper inside as he continued to grow. Bringing my head to the moment we caught ourselves back in. Each thrust made me realize that I wouldn't be able to walk tomorrow. Another push, deeper inside me. Deeper and deeper. *Fuck! Too deep? Fuck.* I pushed him out of me and sat up quickly. He stepped back confused why I stopped him.

"Did I hurt you?" he asked, now with innocence and concern.

"No! Fuck, my pills fell out of my purse yesterday and went down the sewer, carried away by the rain. The clinic was closed today, so I won't have my birth control back in me until tomorrow," I said, panting between breaths. Pissed off that I ruined the moment, and of course the story sounded made up, but it was true. Juggling my hands with my phone and the stupid manuscript from my boss trying to keep everything dry. Unfortunately, when I reached for a pen in my purse the damn envelope of pills fell out and were washed away in the stream. Just my luck.

Panic rushed across his face. Neither of us could have a child right now.

"Fuck, Ais, why didn't you say something? I could've used a condom."

"I know, I wasn't thinking. Obviously." I waved my arms toward our whole situation that shouldn't be happening. *Damn tequila.*

"Well, I can run to the store right now."

"Just finish fucking me first. You're already inside me, developing a mini you to rule the world," I said, as he laughed.

"Ais, we shouldn't." He hesitated with his dick still pulsing in his hand.

"Just come back and fuck me. We will get the gremlin ejector in the morning after you make me breakfast."

He bit his bottom lip as he debated, but he walked back toward me anyway… and didn't hesitate to thrust back inside me. Making me moan as my orgasm came back, and the blood flowed back to my face as I let out a loud moan and climaxed the last of the energy left in me. I could feel all our future fuckups starting to drip out of me and onto the table. He pushed deeper inside of me one last time before pulling out and grabbing the kitchen towel to help with the mess. *Better on the table than in me.*

"You know, we really gotta stop meeting like this. Starting to think you're stalking me for the sex," he said, as he walked back to me, wiping the table and my legs before pulling my panting body up to him, kissing me softly.

"I. Am. Not. Stalking. You," I said, trying to catch my breath, swallowing hard. "I was out for Lena's birthday party and trying to suck up for a promotion. We just happened to be at the same bar. Again."

"This is three weekends in a row, Ais." He smirked and raised his eyebrow. "It's definitely stalking."

"Are you questioning my truthness right now?" I asked.

He nodded and laughed.

"Well, I fucked two other men this week at the same time. They ran a train on me. Dicks everywhere. So, I must be stalking them too, huh?" I winked and started to laugh.

His smirk went away, and the protectiveness I knew too well met his eyes. He closed the distance between us, letting his lips touch mine. He kissed my lips harder, sucking on my lower lip, bruising it with a hickey. Claiming me to be his.

"You fucking better not have," he whispered.

I could see his jealousy rising, and deep down, I loved this side of him. Dominant, knowing what the hell he wanted in life and how to get it. And whenever he tried to control me, it only made me want him more.

I smiled, knowing that I was lying about any other man. To be fair, I couldn't even remember the last time that I had an actual man inside me. My wrist and my pathetic bedside nightstand truthfully thanked him for getting me off. And I was sure the rest of the world that would interact with me over the next few days would be happy to meet this Aisling Lux, and not the sex deprived bitch that I could be.

I stared back at him and watched his eyes study me, and a part of me loved to see this jealous side of him come out and play. He would burn the world down for me, and yet I wouldn't even let him take me on a proper date.

"You tell me, was my pussy as tight as last weekend?" I smirked.

He took his fingers and pushed them deep inside me, pulling me toward him with his other hand. "This is mine. Only mine. I don't share," he growled.

"Mmmm. Now there's the man that I would marry," I whispered back to him, whimpering as I came to another high and let my confession slip out. "I'm only yours," I whispered. Knowing that as much as I wanted to have control over my emotions for him, I couldn't stop myself from catching feelings the more time we spent more time together. I kissed his neck as he played with me, and I knew that this was the start to a whole lot of shit. If he were as smart as New York's magazines said he was, then he would already have one foot out the door and be heading as far away from me as possible.

I smiled when his closeness brought the blood rushing back to my cheeks. There was something about my sex life versus my daily life, though. When I'm being fucked, a whole new person comes out of me and afterwards I'm back to the boring, quiet me. Why couldn't I be sex powerful all the time? Or again, maybe it's the Tequila. I laughed to myself.

"Go clean up in the shower, I'm running to the store. Chocolate chip or banana pancakes?" he asked, as his fingers were still inside me and his thumb rubbed my pleasure pebble, making his question irrelevant. *I don't give a damn about pancakes right now.*

"Mmmm," I moaned and shook my head. "You." I moaned louder as I reached another orgasm. I meant to say, you pick, but you, was all I could say and I think he liked that answer even more. He reached for a clean towel and slowly pulled his fingers out of me, wiping them clean.

"That's better," he said with a smirk.

After he cleaned us both up and pulled his shirt over his head. He walked out of the apartment while I laid on the table, still panting.

Chapter 2
Tequila Hangovers

The sun was blinding through the shades, and I wanted to crawl under a dark rock and go back to sleep. I grabbed the blanket and pulled it over my head, then reached for the pillow to add to the darkness. The too many Tequila shots were starting to creep up on me. My stomach started to churn. I took a deep breath in and sat up quickly, as an unfamiliar scent came from my small apartment. Dizzily, I let my eyes refocus.

Pancakes?

I smiled, knowing that Jameson stayed, and then frowned, realizing that last night really did happen. I couldn't keep doing this to him. I couldn't bring him back into my life only to crush him later. He deserved better.

Ugh.

I laid back down and covered my head again to hide the shame that started to consume me. How was I supposed to kick him out of here when he was always beyond good to me?

Shit. I heard the second bedroom door open, and I knew I had to get up now or all hell would break loose.

"The fuck you doing here?" Trevor said, pissed.

"Making pancakes for Ais, what are you still doing here?"

I hurried and ran out to get between them so no one died today in my apartment. The last thing I wanted was to hide a body, and of course, Jameson and I both knew it wouldn't be either of ours.

"Hey, hey, hey," I walked between the two of them. "It's fine," I said, while pushing Jameson back. I could see his jawline harden, and my heart raced as I realized he was ready to fight. "Trevor, this is Jameson, and Jameson, this is Trevor, my roommate."

"I'm her ex-boyfriend, not just a roommate," Trevor interrupted.

"Hold your tongue, Trevor," I said, and added quietly to myself, "if you plan on keeping it."

Jameson's arms clenched as he gave Trevor the death stare.

"Hey, he's just finishing his lease. Look at me." I grabbed his face and made his eyes connect with mine. "He'll be moving out next month."

"I'll move out when you can afford rent without me," he interjected.

"Today," Jameson said and pushed past me. "She can pay it in full, today. Get your shit, and get out."

"Jameson, stop. He will be out next month. I don't need your help. I'm taking care of things."

"This piece of shit is the bossy ex, huh?" Trevor said, inching his way closer, eyeing him up, and I could see he thought he could win against him. Before I could do anything more, they were inches from each other.

I took a deep breath in and closed my eyes as Jameson's fist met Trevor's face, sending them into a full on brawl in the middle of my small kitchen. The fucking coffee pot shattered, then the table that was used in better form last night became the next victim as Jameson lifted Trevor off the ground and threw him down onto it. I stepped back quickly to avoid any wreckage flying my way, then stood and just shook my head.

"That's enough, for fucks' sake." I jumped in between the two grown men and felt like I was dealing with children. Trevor was trying to stand in the wreckage as I shoved him back down, and Jameson froze as I stood between the two, not daring to lay a hand on me. "Enough," I said one last time, letting them both know that I meant it.

"Today," Jameson huffed, as he caught his breath and pulled out a wad of cash from his wallet, throwing it at Trevor. "You're out today."

Trevor wiped the blood from the back of his head and nodded. He picked up the cash and walked into his half empty room, knowing he had been living with his new girlfriend for the past two weeks anyway. He grabbed his already packed backpack and his toothbrush before scanning the place one last time. The only thing that was actually keeping him here was purposely pissing me off with his presence. I truly did want him out six months ago, but then the promotion didn't go through, and the dating life fell to shit. And a New York apartment was not very affordable on a single income budget. Basically, six months ago, my life started to spiral again.

"Aisling, have fun with that one," he yelled, as he walked past us.

"Bye, asshole," I said, as I grabbed Jameson's arm and hushed him as he went to go after him. "Let him go."

"Why are you dating guys like that?"

"Guys like what?" I asked, now annoyed at him thinking that he could tell me what was right for me.

"You deserve better."

I shook my head, knowing that I'd ruined enough in my life to know that Trevor was exactly the piece of shit I deserved.

"Trust me, I don't."

He grabbed my arm and turned me, lifting my face to his, trying to find the words to say.

"Would you sit down? Your lip is bleeding." I grabbed his arm, pulled him toward the broken table, and made him sit in the chair, grabbing the med kit and walking back to him.

"Thank you for breakfast," I said, trying to change the subject. I looked over and realized the pancakes had ended up on the floor during their brawl. He looked over and laughed.

"Guess I get to take you out on that date anyway. Breakfast it is." He smiled with his broken lip and reached in his pocket, grabbing the pill from the store and handing it to me. "But first, this."

I took the pill and examined it closely before smirking and dropping it on my tongue. I took the glass of orange juice that was still standing on the counter and swallowed it quietly along with my pride.

He would never know the truth, and I planned on keeping it that way. I held back a tear that was trying to reach the corner of my eye and swallowed that back too. If only I could tell him our past, but our past would have ruined our future. I just needed to gently cut him off now and start getting my life back on track, and maybe find a new roommate. Female, preferably, this time.

"I actually have to get to work." I grabbed the top pancake from the stack that landed on the ground and shoved it down my throat. "This is delicious." I winked and kissed him on the cheek before walking to the bathroom to get ready for work. I waited until I heard the door open and close before I inhaled heavily and stared into the mirror at the girl staring back at me, some days I didn't even recognize myself. Plus, no amount of concealer would cover up the drunk tequila bags under my eyes today, and I was ready to be fired from the publisher for losing the manuscript last night at the bar.

Chapter 3
For Fucks' Sake

Could today get any worse? Here I was, standing in my little office, biting at my nails, hoping that the sun would go behind the clouds and let my eyes heal from this hangover. I grabbed the blinds and twisted them hard, until the sun disappeared fully.

"Ugh." I sat down in my creaky office chair and spun around to grab the bottle of water from a week ago and chugged it. I just needed to recover from another weekend spent in the arms of a man I shouldn't be connecting with again. How could I ever tell him about that night? *It would break him.* It still broke me to think about it. I had to stop thinking about it. *Stop it, Ais. Focus.* I opened the bottom drawer and grabbed the bottle of medications that would surely help my head from pounding. Untwisting it quickly, not caring that the cap flipped off and went under the desk, never to be seen again, I popped one, then two and laid my head on my desk, waiting for Devon to walk in with the information that was undoubtedly leaked from half the bar, which was basically our whole staff here at Mark My Words Publishing.

Then, there it was. The knock that I had been preparing for since the seventh shot of tequila last night, knowing that today I would be fired and lose my apartment and then end up back in Wisconsin with my parents.

Ugh.

"It's open," I said, as I sat up quickly and forced myself to sit up tall and pretend to be stable.

"Miss Lux, good morning. I see that you have decided to join us today for work. Do we need to push the deadline for Marleigh's manuscript back, or are we still on time?" He walked to the blinds and opened them, letting the sun blind me again, making me want to puke. "We both know that you need this book to publish with you as the editor, otherwise this office will stay small, or shrink even more. We can't lose her as our author. Marleigh is the mark of our company. Her business is our marketing."

I hesitated for a minute before I realized he didn't know about the manuscript being misplaced yet, because if he did, then he would be furious and ringing my neck across this desk. His face would not be so mellow, and his ears would be filled with steam exiting them.

"We are still on time. I have it all under control," I lied, knowing that the manuscript was taken from my purse last night. Probably by that blonde bitch, Lena, who wanted my position to begin with, and now I would have to grovel at her feet and get it back before Devon noticed it'd been missing, or before she showed him. For sure, it would push me past next week's deadline, and then of course, I wouldn't be paid, again. Why did I become an editor at this piece of shit place in the United States? It used to be top five, and now it was ready to go under. I knew the pressures here would be too much, and I just couldn't resist screwing myself over even more.

"Good." He smiled, which brought me back to reality as he walked out of my closet sized, shitshow of an office. I jumped up and closed the blinds again before I slumped back down into my chair.

"Aisling, there's a man on line five for you. Shall I send him through?"

"Who is it?"

Sarah, my assistant, hesitated. Her hoity, toity, nineteen-year-old, perky self, hoping to catch a break in New York and make it big on her modeling career. But instead, she was too busy fucking her deadbeat guitarist boyfriend from a band that would go nowhere and covering her bruises with high quality makeup. She deserved better. She was too sweet and too smart for him. I listened to her exhaled nervously as I waited.

"He won't tell me."

"Sarah, I don't have time to talk to the press today about anything. If he won't say, then I won't answer."

"Well, Miss Aisling, he's called six times already since you walked in. What do you want me to say?"

"Hang up on the son of a bitch who won't name himself and send him to voicemail." I snapped back, annoyed that I needed to find Lena before she turned me in for losing the manuscript of New York's bestselling author of rich bitches and loose vaginas. I did love her writing, though, and she truly did have a way of making you laugh and cry at the same time. Or maybe it was tears from laughing so hard. But either way, she did know how to keep you entertained, and I loved her entire manuscript that I was almost done editing with before it was stolen.

"Miss, he's calling back."

"Ugh, fine. Send him through."

Sarah transferred the call as I answered the phone, annoyed and ready to raise hell.

"Aisling Lux, how can I help you?"

His voice came through on the other line, and my body froze, everything inside me became dead as he said my name. "You can help me with much more than you think."

I couldn't speak as his voice sent shivers down my spine.

"It was nice seeing you last night," he inhaled slowly. "Unfortunately, you went home with my brother, and that I don't like."

"Jared," I said. "What do you want?" Trying to keep my temper from emerging, I knew the ripple effect that he could cause in my life right now.

He inhaled slowly again as if imagining me naked in front of him while he tore my clothes off, and sadly, I knew the shame all too well because I was the one that let it happen. Out of sadness, disgust, and anger that Jameson had found someone new in his short time away. Had I known that she had just been the hired help for the front page of New York's magazine to finally get the most successful twenty-two year-old duo on the front page… I shook my head, remembering that stupid night ten years ago, and even today, I couldn't get the nerve to tell Jameson about the unfortunate weekend with Jared.

"I have something that belongs to you." He waited for me to process. "My girlfriend, Lena, actually. Sneaky little bitch, she is. I'm assuming you want it back?"

I gasped as I started to put the pieces together from last night, who was at the bar and why they were at the bar. Then I realized, it was for Lena's birthday and this was the Jared that had started fucking her a month ago. Conveniently in New York, ten blocks from where I live and around the corner from work.

I gritted my teeth and swallowed my pride. "I swear, if you so much as lose a page of that manuscript I will–"

"You will do nothing, or I will tell my brother of our little secret."

I hesitated, knowing how vindictive he was, and I knew that he would take any chance he could to try and ruin Jameson's image. If Jameson knew what happened, he would surely kill him and lose everything he worked so hard to build. Jared always felt like he was in his brother's shadow, and when I opened my legs to him, it became a whole new ballgame. Of course, I only let it happen out of anger and then felt the shame coursing through my body. I cried the whole way home, even the whole month after. Which then began my downward spiral. Jared was poison in this world. Charming but poison to anyone or anything he touched. I almost felt sorry that Lena would spiral after him, but at the same time, happy that her karma would finally come back for her the way she deserved. She was awful, but not nearly as awful as Jared.

He cleared his throat, bringing me back to this moment.

"Jared, I'm going to ask you one more time. What do you want?" I held my ground and let the words flow with power that I thought I had.

"Aisling, it's simple. I just want you."

I could see the smirk across his face growing as he knew that he had me right where he wanted me.

Desperate.

I grabbed the phone and slammed it into the base, breaking the handle as I let my rage come through. One single mistake had ruined my life and my future all because of a stupid, young mistake that he would dangle over my head forever now. Of course, it needed to be kept a secret from Jameson, for both his brother's life and my heart's sake.

I knew Jameson would shatter if he knew the truth, and even worse if he knew the whole truth. Back then I needed him to leave and be successful. I needed him to get out of that small town and make it big, where he belonged. Little did I know that I was going to end up in the same big city as him, a decade after parting ways, after I brutally sabotaged our breakup.

"Miss Aisling, is everything okay?" Sarah had walked in without me noticing and was standing in front of me, my head down and the broken phone in front of me. I looked up slightly, wanting to bury myself under this desk forever.

"If I say yes, will you leave me alone?"

She nodded and walked away looking defeated, as if the only thing she wanted was to please others. I put my head back down and let the tears fall, knowing that the manuscript would be with Lena now, and Jared would not give it back without problems added to my plate. *There goes this job.* It had started off as a dream job, and now it was just another nightmare in my spiral of bad luck.

"Miss Aisling, here is a new phone and a cup of coffee. Two sugars with vanilla and caramel creamer, just as you like it. And if I may, don't ever let a man make you cry again. You are better than any of them," she whispered before walking out of the office.

I looked up to an empty room and was thankful for it, but her words sat with me a little longer. She was right. Letting Jared make me cry was a mistake, and I was going to get my manuscript back today, whether I had to deck him in the face or go through Lena. I didn't like either idea, but I didn't have any other choice.

My cell rang, making me jump as I straightened myself and flipped my switch again to the not caring woman that would get what she wants. *I could handle this.*

"Hello?" a man's voice answered sweetly, and I instantly regretted answering the phone. Knowing, again, that yet another man was too good for me, and I shouldn't lead him on when I didn't want anything more from him.

"Hi, Cameron. How are you?" I answered.

New York's own famous billboard lawyer that had been asking for one date with me ever since our coffee run in right down the street. He accidently grabbed my iced coffee with three pumps of caramel, one pump vanilla, cinnamon topping, and two sugars, which then led us to talking for over an hour about the chaos of life, busy jobs that didn't let us breathe, and why my coffee order was so specific.

"I was hoping that you would finally take me up on my offer. Tomorrow night. Eight o'clock?" His deep voice made me quiver, wondering what Jameson would think of this date. Cameron was a muscular man who had to workout daily because his build matched his deep voice. "I'm guessing your silence is you clearing your schedule as we speak to accompany me?"

I cleared my throat and blushed, bringing myself back to reality. A date would be good for me. A date with someone outside of Jameson would be exactly what I needed to get him off my mind. Jameson and I could never be together again. There was too much history between us, and some history needed to stay buried.

"Yes, I am free," I said the words, feeling a weight becoming heavier on my shoulders as to what I was going to tell Jameson later today. "Eight is perfect.

Where should I meet you?" I exhaled slowly, trying to relax.

I could picture him smiling on the other end of the phone with the win. "I can pick you up."

"That won't be necessary. I live in the middle of the city, parking outside my building is impossible."

"I have reservations for The Mirage, I really have no problem picking you up."

I imagined the night before when Jameson picked me up and laid me on the kitchen table. Blushing as I could feel Jameson's lips on my body again, the memory washed over me. *Damnit, Ais, clear your head.*

"Oh, wow," I said with shock at my own thoughts and the quick reservations to the restaurant that was far out of my league. "I will be there, I promise."

"See you then."

I hung up the phone and panicked at the thought of The Mirage being a restaurant that needed reservations months in advance, and now I would definitely need something to wear. We had only met a few weeks ago, and for him to already have a table was either an expensive favor, or he had booked it months ago in hopes of bringing the catch of the month with him. He didn't seem to be a manwhore like that, but it was New York. You never knew.

Grabbing my purse and coffee, I headed straight to Lena's office to confront her.

Chapter 4
You Fucking Bitch

I walked down the hallway to the opposite side of the building and hesitated for a moment. Her small office door was closed, a man's voice talking behind it. I listened carefully, trying to hear if it was our boss getting the truth about the lost manuscript. So, I put my ear closer to the door and waited for more words. Then, I heard giggling and the sound of a smack. Lena laughed as footsteps approached the closed door. I stepped back quickly pretending to get ready with a convincing knock.

The door opened, and there he was. Fucking Jared, standing opposite of me. Lipstick smeared across his neck, and his suit jostled with his tie loosened. The fucking nerve to be in my workplace and calling me. Lena must've stepped away from her office while he pleaded for me to give myself back to him. Obsessive fucker.

"Aisling," he winked, as he opened the door wider for Lena to see me standing there, confidence now gone as anger boiled inside me.

"Do you need something?" Lena asked, as she laughed, wiping the corners of her lips clear of Jared's slobber.

I glared at him as he licked his upper lip before biting his lower one. He leaned against the doorframe seductively, making me uncomfortable at the thought of his tongue inside me a decade ago. I had not seen him for years, even though he wouldn't stop late night calling and texting me. Always obsessing over me or Jameson's business successes. He would send me an updated list of each business that Jameson bought and would pretend to be proud, but instead, he was just doing it to throw it in my face that no matter how successful Jameson became, he would never want me back if he knew the truth. He just couldn't leave me alone and move on. Even while with Lena, she had no idea the amount of time he spent trying to weasel his dirty self back into my life. Jameson would kill him if he knew. I just didn't want to cause the family peace to finally break. The two of them growing up were assholes to each other. Fist fighting everyday over stupid shit. Best decision Jameson ever made was to get away from this psychopath.

"Hello, earth to hungover, drunky," Lena announced her presence again. "What do you want?"

I didn't want to cause a scene with the door to her office wide open and others listening from down the hall. So, I decided to bite my tongue and walk away. Holding the tears back until I could reach the elevator. I walked quickly to leave and clear my head. Best part about editing at Mark My Words Publishing was that Devon lets us leave to work on our projects and get inspiration as long as we kept our phones on and stayed close to the office for communication. But we were able to come and go as we pleased, as long as our work was up to par. Which was why Lena wanted Marleigh's editing gig so badly. She wanted to have ultimate freedom. I only had it from the few magazine articles I helped with, making Devon trust me and my work. This manuscript was my first big job with a deadline, and if I could make it happen, then I would be able to move into the big office next to his as his main editor. Sally was on her way out for retirement, and I so badly wanted it to be the one to take over for her. It was my dream job. But of course, half the company wanted it, so they all wanted to see me fail. My mind raced as I debated on breaking into Lena's apartment to take it back. The elevator door opened, and there he was again. Still smirking.

"Jared, get the fuck away from me." I pushed past him and reached the doors to freedom.

He ran up next to me and grabbed my arm, squeezing it tighter than I had anticipated. I pulled my arm back, trying to get away from his touch.

"Hey, stop being a bitch. I came here to help you." He released my arm and stepped in front of me.

"You have done nothing to help me." I glared at him.

He laughed. "I can get you the stupid papers back. Come on, let's go to her apartment."

I stepped back, arms crossed, and waited for his demands.

"All you have to do–"

And there it was. I pushed past him with a sneer and a right hook that I wished I could have plunged into his fucking face. He would blackmail me into doing something for my dream job's work. "Ugh, get away from me." I walked faster, trying to get as much distance between us as possible. If the world could have divided at this very moment, pulling us into opposite directions, then I would forever be grateful to the higher powers for keeping him away from me.

I was only a block away from my apartment now and debated on running to it to get inside faster or pacing myself to keep my cool.

My arm was grabbed again, stopping me in my tracks as panic consumed me. I was spun around, pinned up against the building wall, making my entire body want to scream to get out of his touch. His lips crushed down onto mine, making me want to vomit. I felt violated. My hands held tight together, making them defenseless against his grip. Anger flowed through me as I remembered his touch years ago, making me lift me knee and jab him hard as fuck in the stomach, pushing him away. "I said get away from me."

I gasped as I realized it was not Jared.

"Oh my god, Jameson, I'm so so–"

"Damn, Ais, who are you pushing away?" He rubbed his deep chiseled abs and looked up and down the street, confused. "I saw you walking as I was getting ready to leave your place. I was hoping you had changed your mind on having a late breakfast with me." He laughed as he shook his head, even more confused at the empty sidewalk.

I felt my face become ten shades too bright as I tried to quickly wipe the single tear that had formed out of anger when I thought Jared was invading my space again. I quickly moved my hand from my face as I looked back into his genuine eyes. His smile faded as he studied my face. His playfulness became serious very fast as the blood rushed to his veins on his forearms and started to pulse as his hands balled into fists at his side.

"Who the fuck hurt you today?"

"No one," I lied, shaking my head, not wanting him to ruin his image over his ignorant, asshole brother.

"You're lying," he waited for the truth while rubbing his fists into a more approachable manner. "Fine, I won't pry," he hesitated before grabbing my hand and walking back with me into my apartment in silence.

I stared in disbelief at the now cleaned up fighting arena. I gasped as I looked around and saw everything was picked up, including the broken table that was no longer in the kitchen.

"I ordered you a new table," he said, as his arm went to the back of his head, rubbing his hair, letting his hips show from under his shirt. At that moment, he seemed so shy with me, but I knew him too well to know that he was very confident of himself, or at least his body. "It was time for a new one anyways." He sat down at the lonely chair that was left after the brawl broke the others.

He patted his thigh in demand for me to come and sit. But today had been a shitshow already, and I was ready to break. I couldn't lean into him for comfort right now. I needed to give myself space. I couldn't drag him down with me in my own personal spiral.

I smiled and walked past him into the bathroom to take a long hot shower.

Alone.

I turned the faucet on and let the room fill with aromas of peaches and tea tree oil, letting the cool, calm mix fill my lungs and my body tingle from the sensation before getting naked and staring at my broken self in front of the mirror before the steam covered the entire reflection. I pointed to myself in the mirror and made my demands, "You're going to fix this, all of this," before jumping into the shower.

I let the tears flow and wash themselves away with the water. I heard the door creak open as Jameson walked into the bathroom. I watched above the shower liner as his arms came up and his shirt came off over his head, and I heard his jeans unzip. I inhaled slowly, trying to slow my breathing. I wanted him close to me, even though I knew that he deserved better. It was my own sickness and lies that made me want to push him away. A set of demons trying to tear my entire life to pieces. But they were my own and made up in my head.

Because everything always felt right around him, and I hated that I would destroy him. I was just too much of a coward to tell him of the big elephant in the room staring at me. My hands went to my stomach as I felt the emptiness inside me. I dropped my hands and closed my eyes as I imagined how life would have turned out differently if I just would've told him that I was pregnant with his child before I made him move to New York. I just needed him to get away from his poisonous, alcoholic father and selfish, sabotaging brother and for him to succeed and break the mold of the Tonic family curse.

If I would've told him, he would've stayed, and all of his dreams would have been shattered. And of course, him being too good of a guy, he would've stayed and built a home with me and roots for a lifetime, but then he never would've become successful, as he needed to be. He had given so many great opportunities to small businesses to help them grow as their angel investor, and he wouldn't be the millionaire that he is today. All those small-time shops would've been buried by corporations. He did the right thing. I didn't, but that was something that I must live with now, not burden him with.

His arms pulled me into him as he joined me in the hot shower, bringing me back to the reality of his closeness. My head spun at how bad I wish we could make things work. His arms wrapped tightly around me, securing me into him. He kissed my neck slowly as the steam hovered between us. Letting his tongue travel to my collarbone, his lips continued to give me love I didn't deserve, and his hands gently rubbed my arms, trying to soothe me.

"Whatever happened today, I'm going to fix it," he whispered.

I huffed and smiled doubtfully. "It's okay." I didn't need my problems to become his.

"That smile of yours needs to be more visible." His lips met mine as his tongue slipped into my mouth, and he kissed me deeply. His hands caressed me, making my mind stop spinning, and the world became quieter. The perfect distraction for my busy mind. I waited for him to slip his fingers inside me and was ready for the excitement to begin. When his kisses continued but he didn't initiate the next step, I lowered my hand to grab him. He grabbed my hand tight and forced it away from him, groaning as he stopped me and smirked between kisses.

"No." He grabbed the soap and poured it into his hands, rubbing them together to get the bubbles growing. He slowly started to rub my entire body and refused anything back in return. "You need rest," he whispered, as he washed my body. Then, he grabbed my shampoo and began to wash my hair. The sensation of the tingling shampoo and his muscles caressing me while his fingers massaged my head began to make my body quiver. I looked up and waited for his lips to return to me. He kissed my nose and smiled while he rinsed away the dirt and shame and last night's tequila down the drain. He pushed me gently against the shower wall and turned me around to face it. I waited for him to enter me from behind, and when he didn't, I tried to turn back around. He held me still as he poured the conditioner into my hair and massaged it in.

I turned around and laughed. "Are you really not going to fuck me?"

He smirked. "Miss Aisling, is that what you really want, or are you just trying to please me?"

"I mean, I want it too." I laughed.

He rinsed out my hair and kissed my lips gently. "You're clean." He winked as he shut the shower off. He held his dick in his hand and pulled the curtain back to grab the towel. He wrapped it around me before pulling me to his still naked body. His dick was very hard and touched the middle of my back. Full well knowing that he wanted me too, I blushed as it rubbed against me. He lifted me up and carried me to my bedroom, laying me down on the already made bed.

He opened the nightstand and grabbed a condom from the top drawer, ripping it open with his teeth and pulling my body closer to the edge of the bed while getting himself ready to enter me. I lifted my lower half up toward him. He leaned over me and grabbed the pillow from the head of the bed and laid it underneath me, raising my hips high, before gently thrusting into me.

Today was different than last night. Today, he was taking his time, mapping out my entire body as the towel fell off my nipples. He stood tall and let himself move in and out of me, each thrust making my entire body fill with warmth as the tingling from the tea tree soap continued to grow on me. The sensation of him watching me and the warmth with cooling sensations was all too much, and within a matter of seconds, I could feel my climax coming to its peak. He grinned his brilliant smile as he saw it too. He leaned in closer to me, lifting my entire body to his and finishing with me with my legs wrapped around his body and his dick left pulsing inside me.

Panting, he slowly laid me back down onto the bed and turned to get rid of the filled condom. He walked back over and laid next to me, on top of the covers. He pulled me closer to him, my back to his abs as he kissed the back of my head and spooned me until I fell asleep in his arms, dreaming of the what if's that could've, should've, and would've been if I had just told him the truth.

Chapter 5
Date Night

My eyes opened, and I reached for my phone to check the time. I was a little shocked when I noticed I was alone in my bed. I sat up with the covers now on me and looked around the room.

"Jameson?" I whispered, afraid that he might've finally taken the hint and ran from me, and also sad that I knew it was for the best.

He walked back into the room with angered eyes. I sunk back into the bed, praying that Jared had not stopped by while I was sleeping. I grimaced, waiting for my punishment of whatever news he knew of. My phone in his hand.

"You can't go on a date with him," Jameson said.

"You went through my phone?" I asked, irritated at my privacy being invaded.

"What? No, of course not. Cameron called several times, so I finally answered. He's insisting on picking you up for your date tonight and asked for your address. I told him you would call him back."

"Tonight?" I grabbed my phone and panicked. "I slept the whole day and night? Oh my god. I have so much work to do, and now I wasted a whole day."

"Well, I wouldn't call it completely wasted." He smirked at my naked body.

"Okay," I laughed, "Not wasted. I just have a deadline."

He nodded. "The manuscript for Marleigh Englewood. Yes, that is going to be the book of the year." He hesitated while glancing around the room for the booklet. "I can go through a few chapters today to help catch you up."

"No, I need to do this on my own. I just need to find it first." I froze as I said too much.

"Find it? Ais, what happened?" Concern crossed his face.

"My bad day yesterday, started with that. I will fix it."

Jameson shook his head. "I know you will. I just hope you don't have to break any bones to do it." He laughed and sat next to me on the bed. "Now back to business. You can't go on a date with Cameron. He's not good enough for you."

I laughed. "Are you kidding me? He deserves better than me." I pushed my hair behind my ear and blushed at not meaning to say the words out loud. "Plus, I don't need your permission," I spat back, trying to feel powerful again.

He put his finger over my lips and hushed me. "I don't like it."

"You know him personally?"

He nodded as he stood and walked to the other room before coming back into the bedroom. "Fine, I give you permission to go on a date with him, but you have to wear these."

He pulled out a pair of laced panties with a small pocket in the front and tossed them to me.

"And what am I supposed to do with these?" I twirled them around my finger. "I wasn't planning on wearing any."

He glared back at me before he pulled out a small metal object and smirked. "You have to wear those with this, and then I'll let you go on a date. If you decide you still want to be with him while thinking about my dick inside of you, then so be it. I'll leave you alone."

"Do you always carry that around with you?"

He laughed. "I saw it last night when I went to the store for the pill and thought it would be fun." He stood up and kissed my cheek before walking to the door. He turned back and asked, "The Mirage at eight?"

I stared at the panties in my hand and the metal vibrator on the table. He cleared his throat, waiting for an answer. I looked back to him and nodded, speechless, before he walked out and left me alone with my thoughts.

I debated on what dress to wear for the last hour, tossing half my wardrobe onto my bed because every piece I grabbed reminded me of Jameson, and I didn't want to be reminded of him while out with Cameron. I needed to give Cameron a fair shot if I truly wanted to move on. A month ago, meeting Jameson out at the bar had led me straight into a trap. Each time I have been out now, I ended up coming back with him. He literally won everytime.

Fuck it.

I grabbed Jameson's favorite thigh high black lace dress and grabbed my black heels with red soles and stood in front of the mirror while still debating on the panties, but ultimately, my mind was already made up. I was going to wear them. I was excited to see what they could do, and the excitement was exactly what I needed.

I slipped them on and stood waiting for them to work.

Nothing. He gave me a fucking broken vibrator.

I laughed while standing in front of the mirror. "That's what you get for a cheap checkout decision." I shook my head, "Asshole."

Grabbing my keys and clutch, I walked downstairs to call a cab that I insisted on taking to the restaurant, in spite of what Cameron wanted. Plus, I needed a few more minutes to collect myself.

Cameron was such a gentleman, waiting outside The Mirage just as we agreed to. I stepped out of the cab, and he ran over to me, trying to hold the already opened door for me. It was a sweet gesture, but not needed.

"Aisling." He smiled and became more handsome in the city lights, his green eyes glistening. I blushed at how I could even be so lucky to have landed this model of a man with a sweet soul.

"Oh, thank you."

He insisted on paying the cab driver as I stepped out and wouldn't take no for an answer. His hand reached behind my lower back and gestured us into the restaurant.

"Good evening, reservation?" a dark brunette bombshell asked, annoyed.

"Yes, Cameron Smith."

The lady looked up and smiled, changing her demeanor real quick when she noticed the man's beautiful face standing in front of her, before glaring at me. She must've recognized his face from the billboards outside for marketing as the number one lawyer here in all of New York after winning a number of celebrity cases.

"Oh, I'm so sorry, sir, this way please. We have the sky deck all ready for you two. There will only be four other tables up there tonight. So, privacy will be at its best."

"Thank you, miss," he answered sweetly.

I walked around the roof of the restaurant in awe of the stars shimmering brightly above us and the city lights surrounding us all the way to the state borders. It was absolutely breathtaking for a New York view at night. Truly magical in this busy city.

"Wow, I never knew this place could look so beautiful and peaceful," I said, admiring the view.

"You make it even more beautiful standing here. Wow, Aisling. You are stunning." He came close to me and kissed my cheek, making me blush. "Shall we?" he gestured toward the reserved table with champagne sitting in the ice bucket. I nodded as we walked toward the table. He pulled my chair out and let me sit. I was thankful now that these panties were pointless, this man was too nice and I shouldn't fuck it up this time.

The waitress came around as he began to pop the cork off the champagne. She smiled and waited for him to finish, so as not to get a black eye by the end of her shift. I laughed silently to myself at the idea since I could see she already hated that I was with this man tonight. She smiled at him and then glared back at me. *Ugh.* Women.

"What can I get started for you?" she asked Cameron, ignoring me.

He picked up the menu and said, "We will start with the oysters and calamari. Then, we will have the chef's special from the hidden menu please."

"Great choice, sir, I will tell the chef." She winked and walked away.

"The chef's special?"

"You will love it," he fidgeted in his seat, nervously. "I hope that's okay that I ordered for you? I just knew that you hadn't been here before, and I didn't want you to be disappointed."

I blushed because I was actually happy that I didn't even have to look at the menu or the prices because I was pretty sure that at a place like this each meal would be my entire week's pay. I just wanted to split the bill at the end, swallow my pride silently, and make ends meet by picking up a bartending shift with Sarah next weekend at her parents' bar if I needed to.

"Thank you," I smiled and looked over at the city lights again. "I just can't get over this view, it's so breathtaking." I grabbed my glass of champagne and brought it to my lips, the bubbles tickled as I sipped the liquid. Almost choking, I froze, as my panties started to buzz. My entire body shivered as my pleasure pebble was being distracted. I quickly crossed my legs, trying to settle the vibration, and set my glass down.

"Everything alright?" Cameron asked, concerned.

The vibration continued, and it made my own words incomprehensible for the moment. The buzzing finally slowed as blood rushed to my face, and my entire body shivered with pleasure. I caught my breath quickly before Cameron thought I was having some sort of medical condition that would need further attention. I froze at the thought of a hospital visit, only for them to find a vibrator in my panties and the embarrassment of having to admit the sensation was all coming from another man.

"Never better." I grabbed the side of the table and laughed. "Sorry, the chill in the air caught me off guard for a minute," I lied, as the summer night was warm and humid.

He jumped up without missing a beat, and without questioning my actual body temperature, taking his suit jacket off and bringing it to my shoulders, rubbing my arms to warm them up on my already sweaty body.

Then, I looked up where Cameron had been sitting and gasped, as I saw a man walking straight toward us.

Jameson.

I froze as I watched him slow and take his seat across from us at his own table. Table for one.

Oh. My. God. That fucker!

He smirked and winked as he lifted a mini silver object and waved it in the air. He squeezed his thumb on it, and my panties vibrated again. I clenched my legs together and braced myself. Cameron walked back around, oblivious to the man causing my tremors, and took his seat. Now I was fucking sweating in his jacket.

I glared at Jameson and waited for the pleasure to subside before smiling back at Cameron.

"Thank you." I pulled the jacket on tighter, hoping that it would conceal my tremors of pleasure being caused by the man across the way. I watched carefully as Jameson talked to the waitress. He had two glasses on the table, and when the waitress went to remove one, he stopped her by grabbing her hand gently, and she giggled like the fucking bitch that she was, flirting and trying to leave with him for the night. Now I was glaring at her. I swallowed hard and unclenched my jaw as I was on a date with another man. I knew I wasn't being fair, but he intentionally was bringing another woman on my date night to intrude, and my jealousy started to brew. I tried to shake the feeling, knowing that he deserved to be with someone else just as much as I should let myself do the same.

Cameron turned around and followed my stare. "Do you know the waitress with Jameson?"

Hearing his name from Cameron's lips brought me back to the now, and I froze. "The waitress?" I realized he knew Jameson, and now I wanted to run for the tallest building here and step off. "I, uh, do you know Jameson?"

"We work out together, and he leases me the law firm building. He's the reason I came out to New York. He had clients that needed a great lawyer. Not to brag or anything, but I've never lost a case." He smiled his brilliant, white smile with perfect alignment. His hygienist probably gets wet the moment he sits in her chair. I'm sure she wants him just as all the women here in New York do. And yet, oddly enough he chose to take me on a date. Something must be wrong with him.

"Oh," was all I could say, as my mind raced.

"You have a history with him," he stated.

I didn't want to speak, so instead, I just nodded.

"Ended that badly, huh?"

I shook my head, as the vibrator started to tingle again, making me remember our recent nights together. I pulled tighter onto Cameron's jacket and tried to let my body calm itself. I looked up and smiled, grabbing the glass of champagne and chugging it, using the alcohol as an excuse for the flushed cheeks. "I wouldn't say that." I said, knowing that all of our endings had been orgasmic. I looked past him at Jameson and felt the panties start to vibrate again. "Damn it," I said out loud accidentally before standing up, realizing that I now looked crazy to the entire rooftop. "I'm sorry, I have to use the restroom."

Cameron stood, pointing me into the direction for my escape. I smiled and kissed his cheek, making him blush. I walked past Jameson and flipped him off on my way to the women's restroom. I heard him laugh as I quickly pushed the door open and ran into the first open stall and slipped the thong off with the vibrator. I sat down on the toilet to steady myself and laughed knowing damn well that Jameson knew exactly what he was doing when he made me the offer. He wanted to sabotage my date, he wanted to keep my mind on him, he wanted to ruin me more than I was already ruined.

I grabbed the panties and shoved them in the jacket pocket before straightening myself and stepping out from the stall. Walking to the mirror and fixing my flushed face with a little bit of foundation and lipstick, I took the jacket off and slipped it over my arm as I headed for the door. It opened as Jameson's waitress bumped into me.

"Oh, I'm so sorry." She grabbed my arm and helped straighten me. "Oh, you dropped these." She reached down to grab the black panties and froze when she realized what had fallen out of the jacket pocket. I quickly swiped them up and laughed.

"Thanks." I winked at her and walked out. I walked back to my table with confidence and my panties in hand. Passing Jameson on my way, I bunched the panties into my hand with the metal bullet and dropped them in his lap, then walked back to my table with Cameron.

I smiled when I sat back down and watched Jameson's expression change from happy to anger as he realized his fun distraction would be over for the night.

"Where were we?" I asked Cameron.

He smiled and started to discuss his happiness for me accepting tonight's date. He poured another glass for me as the food arrived. I winked back at Jameson one last time before I let my focus remain on the wonderful man that brought me out tonight.

"It looks perfect, thank you," he said to the waitress before she even asked. She smiled at him and returned to her quarters.

Cameron moved his chair to the side of me, instead of across. Leaving us wide open to Jameson's full viewing pleasure. It was unintentional to Cameron, and I silently laughed to myself at the decision. It was only fair for him to get tortured after making me tremble in my seat for the first half.

I looked up slowly and smirked at Jameson as I leaned in closer to Cameron and let him feed me the oysters and giggled while we discussed everything and nothing. I could feel Jameson staring at my now open neck and chest with the jacket off and exposing my skin to the cooling air. Cameron continued to inch his way closer to me and I watched as Jameson squirmed in his chair. I swore he almost stood up at one point when he watched as Cameron wiped oyster juice from my chest after it spilled when he lifted it for me to suck down.

I didn't know what was turning me on more, the fact that Cameron was actually very romantic and sensual or the fact that Jameson would surely end up in my apartment tonight, whether that was a good thing or not, I was still unsure about it. His jealousy could be intense unless he matured more since a decade ago. He would surely try to claim me as his for tonight after all of this. Or at least I fantasized that it would happen. As shitty as it sounded in my own head, I knew Cameron was great, but Jameson was Jameson. We had history together, and that's hard to let go. Maybe the best decision was to leave both of these men alone and move out of New York if he was planning on staying here.

I looked up and froze as I saw Devon walk across the rooftop toward Jameson. He stood up and reached his arm across the table, shaking Devon's hand and pointing to the open chair with the empty glass.

"Sorry I'm late," was all I heard him say, as the music on the rooftop turned up, and their conversation disappeared.

For the next hour, my nerves started to get the best of me. What was he doing here with Jameson? Did he find out about the manuscript? Was he firing me?

Let it go.

I stopped analyzing and came back to the now and poured another glass of wine. We were going to need another bottle at this rate.

"Cheers to the most beautiful woman in New York," Cameron announced, as our glasses clinked.

Guilt started to build inside me that part of me was using him for revenge against Jameson, but had he never given me those panties, then this date would have ultimately been perfect. Cameron deserved better than me. I would only bring him down into my spiral as I would with Jameson too. I did not deserve this man nor any man right now. I needed to finish my manuscript and get that promotion, so I had something to be proud of. For myself.

"I think the wine is starting to overtake your judgment." I laughed quietly. "I think it may be time to call it a night."

Cameron looked slightly disappointed but nodded almost immediately. "It's the fresh air and wine. Please tell me that you will let me drive you home? Just to be sure you make it safely."

Guilt built even more now because he was too much of a perfect gentleman for me, a*nd I would destroy him,* my own voice whispered to me. But I watched as his eyes pleaded, and I knew that he was genuine and only wanted my safety. I nodded.

"I would appreciate it very much." I smiled and exhaled slowly. This man deserved better than me.

He insisted on paying for the entire meal and would not argue about it. After the waitress glared one more time at me, we stood and walked to the exit stairs, opposite of Jameson. Not wanting to glance in his direction, knowing that one look from him would make me crumble, I kept my eyes forward. Cameron kept his hand at the small of my back and led me through the restaurant, toward his VIP parked car, opening the door for me and holding my hand as he led me into it.

We pulled up to my apartment, and Cameron jumped out and ran around to my door, opening it. Helping me out and steading myself, he hesitated, and I could see him debating if this was the moment to lean in for a kiss.

He leaned in closer to me, "I'm going to kiss you on the cheek. Maybe on our next date you will let me kiss you for real."

I blushed as he leaned in, and I could feel the heat of his body mere inches from me. I nodded and accepted the kiss.

"You are too good for me," I whispered, as he pulled back and studied my expression.

"If I am too good, then your standards are too low." He lifted my chin up and let our faces linger before he kissed my nose and held his hand out for my doorway. "Thank you. Tonight was exactly what I needed."

"No, thank you for everything." I blushed again as I rubbed his hand and walked away from him into my apartment.

Kicking off my heels, I stripped off my dress before laying on top of my covers and replaying the night over in my head. Cameron was great, if only Jameson hadn't shown up three weeks ago and rushed all my feelings back inside me. Why must the timing always be against me in this world?

I pushed myself back against the headboard and crawled under the covers with my phone in hand. I knew I shouldn't, but I just needed to send one text. Maybe it was liquid courage, or maybe it was my own stupidity. I opened my phone with the bright screen blinding me and opened Jameson's contact information and pressed on the text button. I hesitated for a minute before changing my mind and started to close my phone when it chimed.

Jameson: Are you home?

His text made me smile as I realized he would've seen us leave and curiosity got the best of him too.

Aisling: Wouldn't you like to know.
Jameson: Hence why I asked. Smartass.
Aisling: I am home.
Jameson: Alone?

I stared at the text and debated on the right words. If I told him yes, then would he come over? But that would make me feel even worse, knowing that Cameron was such a gentleman, and yet, I didn't even kiss him. He had spent the time and put the effort into setting up the whole night. But then if I tell Jameson that I have company, then who knows what his jealousy could bring. If only he knew how much more jealous I was of him and any possible girl he had been with, that I made mostly up in my head, but still…

Jameson: Ais?

At this point, it was best to not answer him. If I let him come over tonight, then the next thing I knew, we would be dating again. Then our secrets would become just big ass elephants in the room, and I would eventually have to tell him about our unborn child and the encounter with Jared… Now my stomach turned on me, whether it was the wine or the anxiety of the truth. I jumped up and ran for the bathroom before burying my head in the toilet, letting the cold ground become my bed for the night.

Chapter 6
Time To Be a Badass Again

My alarm went off, sending me to sit straight up and reach for my phone, realizing that I spent the night on the bathroom floor. I adjusted my stiff neck and shoulders before I jumped up and ran to my bed to shut the blaring alarm off. My anxiety had consumed me last night, making me sick. The wine was good but definitely not strong enough to make me waste it down the toilet. That was it. I just needed to focus on myself today. No men, no drama. Just get to work on the smaller articles that could be done for now and pretend like nothing was wrong.

I saw my phone had missed calls and texts. I didn't even want to see who they were from because I already knew the name that would be staring back at me, and I could already feel his eyes on me from across town. I tossed it across the bed and grabbed a towel to shower off the old me and be the badass bitch that I was. I quickly got dressed and grabbed the heels from last nigh, deciding to layer with a black blazer to make me feel like a boss for today. I curled a few loose ends into my hair and added red lipstick before leaving my phone ringing for the tenth time on the bed and headed to work. Today's plan was to ignore the world and get my life back on track.

I walked toward the coffee shop where I had met Cameron. I stopped in front of the door and smiled to myself at the smell of success brewing inside the place. I opened the door and smiled at the lady behind the register. She was my favorite one who knew my signature coffee. She waved to me as she turned around to grab my cup to fill before the line of others ordered. When I reached the counter, I quickly tipped the barista specifically as she reached over to hand me my order without me having to say a word.

"Thank you."

"Two sugars with vanilla, caramel creamer, and a dash of cinnamon." She smiled and refused the tip as she got onto the next order. I sipped happily on the hot sweetness as I slipped my sunglasses over my eyes and walked out of the shop to work.

I took a deep breath before reaching the Mark My Words building and hesitated for only a moment before marching in with an attitude that was not going to be disrupted by anyone today. I smirked to myself when I made it to my office peacefully. I closed the door, along with the blinds to the small door window, letting my coworkers know that I was in a do-not-disturb mode. I had shit to get done today and not a lot of time to do it. Tomorrow, I was going to beat Lena's ass in the middle of her office to get my endless hours of hard work manuscript back. I had too many edits already written on the paper copy, and she knew that I didn't have time to start over now. But that was tomorrow's job.

I flipped my laptop open and began on the articles for the small columns magazine and started to edit each line, word for word. A place where I could get lost. Words were my safe zone in this world. Consistent and endless, all at once. One word could completely change the entire story, which made me feel as if I had power to tell the story the way it was meant to be told. I knew this field, and I could live in it forever. Books and writing were the one thing in my life that I never messed up.

A slight knock on the door made me lose my train of thought and float back to reality as Sarah shyly walked in. "I have a gentleman on the phone for you."

I looked up from typing and froze. "I am busy today. Can it wait?"

"He said it's urgent."

"He, as in who exactly?"

My stomach churned as Jared's face came to mind, making me want to grind my teeth.

"Jameson Tonic."

I huffed and laughed. "Not today." I lifted my sunglasses from the table and twirled them in the air as I leaned back into my chair. "I have a career that I am trying to advance in. I don't have time today. Could you relay the message?"

Sarah hesitated and paced the room.

"Sarah," I snapped. "Tell him not today."

She jumped at the sound of her name as if she were in trouble. "It's just–"

"Oh for fucks' sake, what?"

"Did you not read the emails this morning?" she asked.

I looked back down at my open laptop, confused, seeing the inbox button flashing back at me with one unread email waiting to be seen. *Shit*. What was I missing?

"Aisling, he owns our company. I can't really tell him no."

My jaw dropped. "Who owns the company?" I inhaled sharply as I leaned against my desk and moved the mouse over to the inbox, clicking the email, and freezing as I saw his name come across the screen. I looked back up to Sarah and waited for the response that I already knew was coming.

"Mr. Tonic. The email came out this morning at seven. He will be here shortly for the team building meeting with Devon."

"Get out," I snapped.

Sarah froze, and I could see she was building her courage to go against my wishes. I was very proud of her, but this was not the moment to do this. "No, I'm sending him through to you."

"Sarah, don't you–"

Damn it.

She quickly turned on her heel, and within twenty seconds, my work phone started to flash.

That bitch.

I hesitated before lifting the receiver.

"This is Aisling." I inhaled and waited.

"How was your date?" Jameson's voice sternly asked.

I exhaled, "It was nice." *Boss mode, Ais.* "Since when the hell do you have interest in a publishing company?"

He laughed. "Since I like being in charge, I figured what better way than owning my Ais's company."

"How dare–" I replayed his words slowly in my head and realized the meaning behind them. "Wait, my company? What does that mean?" Excitement should've been coursing through my veins, but instead, anger was brewing. "Jameson, what have you done?"

"I will see you in a minute." The line went dead.

I sat back and began to tremble.

He had no idea that I lost the manuscript for Marleigh, our number one author that we profit from, and here, he just bought the company for me to take over. What the hell was he thinking?

I didn't want to own a company. I just wanted to hide in the corner and edit for others. I just wanted to get lost in the words of others and not be in charge.

The door opened as Jameson walked in confidently. His suit pressed, and the gray undershirt tight against his abs. I watched as he walked his way past my desk and met me behind the short table, spinning my chair sideways to face him.

"When I ask if you are alone, you answer. Understand?" The jealousy in his eyes brought back too much history between us. He was so protective of me back in the day that if any man would have come between us, then it would've ended in a brawl. Which was exactly why I never told him about his brother. Jameson would kill Jared and then I would have to live with the guilt.

I swallowed hard and nodded. I stared and waited for his clenched jaw to release. When I saw him finally relax, I stood up against him and leaned against the desk, trying to make myself feel taller and confident. Even though our heights were nowhere near even.

"You wore my favorite dress and made me know you were panty-less and yet ignored me the rest of the night. Do you know how frustrating that was after I bought this company from Devon, for you?"

I blushed as I remembered our little panty drama last night. "First of all, I didn't know any of those plans, and secondly, you didn't play fair at all." I gently pushed his chest back, making his gaze change from my eyes to my hands. I swallowed quickly, "You didn't even give Cameron a chance."

He smirked. "I gave him a chance. I didn't give you the chance."

I could feel my face get hot as the blood rushed to my cheeks. "That," I inhaled slowly, "wasn't fair." I wanted my mind to be strong and resist him with his closeness consuming me and his sandalwood scent pulling me closer in. I wanted him, physically. But mentally, I knew that things were becoming too close, and I needed to push him away. But how the hell would I do that now with him being my boss?

"Next time you go on a date, please don't ignore my calls." He slowly grabbed my hand and rubbed it gently while looking back up to me.

"There won't be a next time." I looked away, annoyed.

Jameson turned my face gently back toward his, concerned. "Did he hurt you?"

I huffed, "No, of course not. I just need to focus on myself right now."

"So, that's why you ignored my calls."

I nodded.

It was the truth. I couldn't involve anyone in my love life right now until I was done with this book for Marleigh. I didn't have the time for anymore emotional damage or pulling at my heartstrings right now. I just needed to get this book completed and out so that my name would finally be recognized by other authors, and hopefully bring more business into the company.

He stepped back as he studied me. "I bought this company for you. Devon was getting ready to sell it to the investor from Brooklyn, who would eventually pull the plug and close the entire building because he's bored." He exhaled. "I know something is wrong with Marleigh's manuscript and that you're not telling me, and that's okay. But as a businessman, I know that Devon is relying on that book to sell for this company to stay afloat. So, think of me as a new investor, and you are taking over Devon's position. You can keep editing, but you will get to choose who you bring in here from now on and get a raise to pay for your apartment without a roommate. Is that okay?"

I looked up to face him with no words. It was truly a dream come true, but honestly, I wanted to earn it myself. I didn't want anything handed to me. Grateful? Yes. But still.

"Jameson, I don't know how to express the excitement that brings me. It's just–"

"I already know." He nodded. "You needed this achievement on your own for your own accomplishment, and now I just interfered with your plans." He grimaced as he put the pieces together.

"I am grateful. I just wanted something to be proud of."

"You have plenty to be proud of." He shook his head as he stepped away from me, pacing. "Fine. It's my company until you decide if you want to take it over, or you decide who is in charge because Devon has been trying to get out for a year now. His heart is no longer with this place."

I nodded and smiled. "Thank you." I walked over to him and stopped his thoughts, stretching on my heels to kiss his cheek. "Thank you, for real, I mean it."

He smiled before he grabbed my face and kissed my forehead, then pulled me in for a hug. "I know you can do everything alone. I just don't want you to think you have to."

"Always so thoughtful," I said while burying my head into his chest, breathing in his calming scent. "Now I really need to get back to work, boss." I pulled away from him and winked.

"Better work that ass off in my company to reach the top." He smirked before walking out of my little office.

A new boost of confidence came over me. I lifted my phone off the receiver and dialed Lena's extension.

"We need to talk."

Chapter 7
Burn In Hell

Lena agreed to meet me at the coffee shop down the block. I grabbed my sunglasses from my desk and covered my eyes before walking down the halls of my building to keep myself on track of my next target. Once I got to the shop, I waved at the barista, who was always one step ahead of me, and nodded to the second cup of coffee for the day. I grabbed the closest table to the exit and sat with my back against it, just in case she decided to screw me over again. Then, I would be able to get the hell away from her before I did something I would regret. Or maybe not at first, but I would regret later or need bail money to get me out of the overcrowded jail.

I turned on my confidence switch, sat with my signature coffee, and stared out the window, waiting peacefully in the sunshine and soaking in the vitamin D that I knew my body was lacking. But nothing was going to ruin this moment. I was in charge, and technically, I could own the company if I wanted to. But I would not play that card unless it was my last resort. Marleigh would have her edited book in one week, and I was going to be sure of it. I was in charge of my own success.

Me.

"So, you do still want it." His voice made my confidence shrink.

I turned quickly to see Jared standing in the exit doorway with my manuscript in hand. I saw my initials in the corner to mark it as my copy. I glared as I stood up in frustration.

"What the fuck are you doing here?" I tried to snatch my hard work from his hands as he pulled it out of my reach, waving his finger in my face and clicking his tongue, as if he were my parent and I the toddler. *Fucker*.

"I had no idea that Jameson didn't know about our encounter." He sat down and waved to the now open seat. His closeness alone was making me want to tremble, but I needed to keep it together. I sat down quietly and glared.

"You would be dead if he knew," I sneered.

He huffed. "And what? You wouldn't like that? Take your little secret to your grave?" he laughed and leaned across the table, closer to me than I ever wanted him again. "You would miss me too much."

I felt my lip twitch in hatred. "No, I'm afraid that your brother would regret it later in life and I don't want him to suffer anymore from you than he already has." I smirked when I watched Jared's smile turn, and he rolled his eyes.

"You are a real bitch, you know that? It's no wonder why he never came back for you. You had to chase after him, again."

I slammed my fists down on the table, spilling my coffee. I didn't turn to look at the audience that started to grow, but I could feel the tables surrounding us watching.

"And just like that I see that he still has your heart on strings." He smirked and wiped the coffee off the table, setting my manuscript down on the cleaned surface. "So, now what's more important? This work, or him?"

I scoffed. "What sick fucking game are you playing?"

His sly smile made my stomach churn. "You can have this back," he slid the manuscript toward me with his hand still holding it tight against the table. "Leave my brother, and be with me."

I choked on my own air. "Fuck you."

"That's exactly what I want. You, all of you, forever."

I felt bile grow in the back of my throat. "Never. And why would you want someone who doesn't want you back? That's torture."

"Why should Jameson get everything?"

"So, it's about revenge. You're sick." I stood and grabbed my half cup of coffee, ready to leave, but I had ammo, and I needed to use it. "Just so you know, I don't need that manuscript anymore. Your brother has already bought the company and made me the owner. So, you can tell Marleigh yourself why Lena did not turn in a completely edited copy before the deadline." I stood, shaking on the inside but concealing my anxiousness as I started to walk toward the door. Knowing damn well that in three, two, one…

"Aisling, wait." His voice cracked as he finally realized that I had the upper hand.

I smiled as I faced the exit and slowed, waiting for him to meet me. I was no longer going to grovel to this man. And after this, it might be time to let Jameson know of the elephant in the room and let him decide Jared's future before he chose to leave me forever. But, in reality, Jameson deserved better. So, letting him go would be the most unselfish thing I could do.

His hand grabbed mine as if I was ready to run. I tried to pull it away, but he held it stronger with his fingers digging into my wrist. I turned and glared at him. "Let me go, now," I threatened.

He loosened his grip as he pleaded for me to sit back down. My barista watched carefully as she had her phone in hand, ready to dial. I shook my head and turned back on Jared.

"I have nothing left to say to you. You stole from me in an attempt to blackmail me with a revenge scheme on your sibling," I said loud enough for the busy coffee shop watching us. Jared looked around the room and lowered his head. "I no longer am falling for your shit." I threw my arm down, making him fully release me. Then, taking my warm half spilled coffee, I tossed it across his chest. "Go fuck yourself."

My barista cheered loudly as the rest of our audience joined her, and I walked out. I hugged myself for standing up to him and smiled as I headed back to my office to gloat in my own victory and confront Lena for setting me up. It was time she knew the type of man she had been letting in her crotch of thorns, but deep down, I knew that even as low as she could be, she deserved better too.

I walked confidently back into the building and marched straight to Lena's office. Her door was wide open as she sat in her chair and sunk down like the coward that she was as I reached her doorway.

"You," I said, pointing as I reached her desk and watched as her fear kicked in, and she began to tremble. She would have read the email by now about Jameson and myself taking over the company. Now she was cowering in her own failure. I stopped pointing and stood in front of her desk with my arms crossed silently.

"Ais, I–"

"Let me guess. You're sorry?"

She nodded and lowered herself further into her chair, trying to disappear.

"Lena, you, for one, deserve better than Jared. He is a piece of shit, and you are way smarter than him." She began to relax her shoulders as if the words shocked her, and as much as I hated her, she was a brilliant editor. That was why we were at each other's throats to begin with. We both had wanted Marleigh's manuscript so bad that when Devon gave it to me, she left that day in tears. "And I would like it very much if you could help revise my edits on that manuscript, and once you are done, then help me with the last few pages. If it's something that you are still interested in?" I inhaled and waited for her response, shocked at the words pouring out of my mouth.

She sat up, eyes wide as her jaw dropped. "Are you serious?"

I exhaled and relaxed. "Well, now that we aren't fighting for the bigger office, I think we can be friends. Under one condition." I smiled when I saw her perk up. "Jared is no longer welcome here. In this entire building. And you would be smart to leave him."

She smiled and stood, walking around her desk. "I will get the manuscript back right now. Again, I am so, so sorry. Thank you." She hugged me and left her office.

I stood awkwardly at the unexpected affection by my nemesis.

I turned around and smiled.

"Hey, Sarah," I yelled from the small office. She ran in and waited for my demands. "Can you move Lena to the bigger office upstairs next to my new office?"

"But I thought you hated Lena?" she raised her eyebrow and waited.

"Friends close, enemies closer." I winked as she smiled and started to pack her office.

"Oh, and, Sarah," I said, as I headed for the door. "You just got a raise. I'll go get it written up right now, and you can meet me in my new office when you're done." I smiled as Sarah grinned from ear to ear. "One more thing. Please get me a new coffee. I dumped my other one on that asshole guy from the other day."

"Good, I'm glad." She laughed and nodded as I walked to the elevator to get to the top floor of Mark My Words Publishing by Aisling Lux.

Chapter 8
Today Is Good

My phone rang once I made it to my new desk, overlooking New York's city lights. I smiled to myself before skipping to my desk happily to answer it.

"This is Aisling Lux, owner of Mark My Words Publishing," I answered, grinning.

"Well, that didn't take long," his voice answered. "I thought you didn't want help getting to the top," Jameson said.

"Well, the top ended up being a better view. I am still earning it. Just moved to a bigger office to do so." I laughed at my day finally going my way.

He laughed back into the receiver. I could hear him inhale slowly. "So, does that mean I can take you out for a celebratory dinner?"

I had not expected a date from him after already getting me out of a huge bind already. Plus, a part of me half expected to be nothing more than a late night fuck. Or maybe that was what I wished I was, because if I let him take me on a date, then eventually, he would want more and my secret would no longer be mine. It would crush him. I couldn't do that right now.

"How about a raincheck?" I asked, trying to avoid a future between us right now until I could build the courage to tell him the truth about our past.

He exhaled slowly. "If that makes you happy."

I waited for him to say more and demand dinner tonight. When he stayed silent, I finally realized the ball was in my court, and I didn't like it. "You're not going to force me as my boss?"

"Do you want me to?" he asked seductively.

"I mean," I hesitated before stopping myself from having to ruin his night with the truth. But eventually, if we were to be more, then he would need to know. "Next week works better for me. I really need to finish this manuscript."

"Great, you got it back then," he answered.

I gasped and became silent.

"Marleigh was my next phone call to save you. We're old friends, of course."

"Don't you dare," I said. "I mean, don't bother her. I'm almost done."

"Alright, alright," he said, laughing. "Get back to work before I fire you." He hung up the phone before I could respond with a smartass remark.

I leaned back in my chair, smiling at the view and peaceful quietness. The laptop on my desk chimed as it reminded me there was plenty of work to be done. I opened it and got to work with a smile.

After a few hours, I knew it was time to head back to my apartment. I would have to stop at the grocery store first to grab some wine and bubble bath to have this celebration to myself. I made a mental note to call my parents on my way home and let them know the good news. They would have something to be proud of and maybe would even make their way out here to visit this year instead of me going back to Wisconsin, to the small town with only one bar and restaurant. Whereas here, we could wine and dine at a different place each night.

The grocery store was busy for the middle of the week, so I quickly grabbed my few items and jumped in line to wait. Now I wished I would've brought my phone with me to pass the time on mindless games. After a little while, I finally left and made my way home, but when I reached my apartment floor, I froze.

Jameson was standing there with a brown paper bag, leaning up against my door. He turned and smiled as I reached the top step. I was surprised to see him. I thought we had a rain check set for next week already. I walked slowly to the door and fumbled, trying to grab my keys.

"Has a week gone by already?" I nervously laughed, full well knowing that he was the reason that my day turned out better, but I just needed to be alone so that I didn't have to ruin tonight with my secret. I blushed as he grabbed the keys from my hand and unlocked the door, letting me walk past him into my apartment.

"You said no, but I know you."

Guilt brewed inside me, my past thoughts overwhelming.

"You should probably leave," I said, laughing but more serious than he knew.

"Never."

I swallowed hard when I knew he meant well by tonight. But now since Jared reminded me of the elephant, I knew I had to tell him, and today had been such a good day. But I couldn't continue to see him and hold this big lie to myself without the guilt consuming me or using the tequila excuse again.

"I just brought you dinner. I won't stay," he whispered, as he walked up behind me and set the food down on the new table that was delivered earlier. My landlord let them in to set it up with my permission. He grazed my skin with his arm and rested his hand on my hip from behind me. I could feel my blood rushing to the surface at his closeness. His sandalwood scent filled my nose as I breathed deeply, letting my mind calm itself.

"Dinner is great, thank you." I turned around. His body didn't budge as I tried to get plates for the meal. His grin took over as his lips came down to mine. My lips followed his as his tongue pushed his way through and made me pull my body closer to him. Wanting him. Needing him. Then, I froze. "Jameson, wait–"

He groaned as he laid his head on my shoulder, my face leaning up and away from him. "What now, baby?"

That was it. The word 'baby' finally made me break. The guilt of holding the secret in for a decade, and now with seeing him so often and letting my legs and heart open back up to him, it was time. I had to tell him everything before Jared did.

I pulled his face to face mine, trying to find the courage that I would need to get through this. Tears filled my eyes, knowing that after tonight, things would be different, and part of me knew that once he knew the truth, he would never want to see me again. Selfishly, this was why I had been quiet the last few weeks. Enjoying his sweetness and safety that I forever wanted, but as of right now, we couldn't keep growing together with these vines trying to prick me on the way to the rosebud.

"Ais, what's wrong?" he grabbed my face and wiped the now flowing tears. "Baby, don't cry. It's okay. Everything is okay."

I sobbed, letting my past catch up with me. I hugged him tight to hide my tears and enjoy the last few moments of peace before chaos came to the surface. The silence grew, and I could feel his worry strengthen as he waited patiently for me to catch my breath.

I looked up and began, "I have to tell you something."

He wiped my tears and nodded. "Anything."

I frowned, knowing that I was about to break his heart.

"Ten years ago–" I started.

"No, don't do this," he interrupted. "The past is the past. We were different people back then."

I nodded, covering his mouth and making him listen. "Ten years ago, you were flying to New York in a leap of faith as a brilliant twenty-two year-old mathematical genius to become the millionaire investor that you are today. A successful man from a small shithole town, and an even shittier family that would've dragged you further down."

He laughed. "Good riddance."

"Well, the week before you were leaving, we had decided that we would stay in touch, but if an opportunity presented itself, that we would go separate ways. If we found each other again, then we would go from there. We didn't want to hold each other back from success." He nodded as we both knew the rules. "Well, I found out I was pregnant the next week after we made our pact." His confused eyes met mine. "I debated on telling you, but I knew that you would blow the opportunity of your lifetime and stay. So, I decided to wait. I wanted to make sure you moved out of there and were thriving before telling you. I had planned on meeting you out here and exploring New York for myself."

He looked down at my flat stomach and brought his hand to set on it, disbelief growing.

"Mine?" he asked, still looking down. But I could see the vein in his neck pulsing faster.

I nodded, "Yes, you called me, and you were so excited to be out of 'the shithole' and the pure excitement you had after only a week of being away made me wait again. Knowing that if I told you then, you would fly right back home and settle for the small town that you hated, and I couldn't let you do that."

"That wasn't your choice to make." He looked up with sad eyes. "I would've moved you–"

"No, I would have been in the way. We made a pact to explore life, and you needed to focus on your career. I had nothing else going for me, I could handle our baby back home for a little while I thought. Our phone calls kept becoming less and less, and I assumed you were busy with work. Then, the few times you would call, I wanted to tell you, but I was truly afraid of the outcome."

"I was working night and day–" I covered his mouth to keep my courage going.

"You seemed so happy and so successful so fast that I didn't want to ruin it. I was about eighteen weeks along when I knew I had to tell you. I had finally felt her move for the first time, and I needed someone to be excited with. It was a moment that I was so happy that I needed to call and tell you everything. I was going to make you promise to stay focused, and she and I would meet you out here soon."

"The phone call didn't go as planned," he answered.

"You were with a woman." I wiped my eyes as the memory of that fucked up night came to mind. "A supermodel colleague had your attention, and the phone calls became less and less. And each time that we talked, she was always next to you, and the photos in the magazines were all with her."

"It was a business deal."

"Well, I know that now, but when I heard her in the background at midnight, I assumed otherwise," I said, as he shook his head. "I hung up the phone and needed to get out of the house that night. Actually, I felt like I needed to get out of town. My emotions were all over. I thought that I had waited too long and stupidly pushed you away. I cried, thinking that I had lost you. Before I could even reach the car, I slipped and fell on the stupid Wisconsin ice during the winter. Hitting my head, unconscious."

"It wasn't just a concussion." He swallowed hard. "You lost her." His eyes filled with tears, letting his emotions get the best of him.

I exhaled slowly and knew the worst was yet to come. I nodded.

"Babe, I would've been there for you, you should've told me. How could I ever be mad at something like that? You suffered in silence on my behalf." He shook his head in anger. "This was my fault. I never should've left. I would have been there with you. With her." His hand went to my empty stomach as he processed everything.

"Jameson, there's more, and this is where you will hate me."

He looked up, confused. "I could never hate–"

"Damn it, just let me say it. You can leave me after. I just have to get it off my chest."

He stepped back and looked away to hide his own tears while he waited patiently.

I inhaled sharply, "Your brother," his glistening eyes flashed quickly back to me, "was at your parents' house when I had stopped over a few weeks later to grab the rest of my things. He decided to gloat about how you were fucking that 'hot ass' colleague and how he couldn't wait for you to bring her back home to meet her. He showed me the front page of New York magazine of you and her dressed up and attending the gala together. Anger and emotions from the hormones were damaging me inside, and I was sickened knowing that the woman's voice now had a face for me to hate. The paparazzi did a great job of catching every loving angle of you two. Jared decided to tell me your whole dating life while in New York. He told me about the late night fucks and every detail with everyone."

Jameson's eyes became angry, and I was afraid to keep going. "I never fucked anyone. You were all that was on my mind."

I ignored him, feeling the guilt even harder now, hearing the truth from him.

"I was so angry at you and the world. Jared was there… and I needed a distraction. Anything to make me feel something again. Whether it be hate, love, revenge. I just needed something, and you weren't there. You were off fucking her I thought."

"I never fucked her," he growled before reaching me and pinning my arms to my side. "Ais, I never had anyone back then. It was you, it was always you."

The tears flowed as I knew I had to finish the disaster now.

"Jared was there for me. He–"

"Don't you fucking say it, Ais. Don't." He pushed back away from me. His heart breaking in front of me as his mind wandered and relived the night I tried to push back and bury myself.

"I let him fuck me, I asked for it. I hated you that night. Hell, I hated Jared that night. I hated the woman that took you from me. Then, afterwards, I cried the entire drive back home, knowing that he had just manipulated me into what he'd been wanting for years. To break you."

"You fucking didn't. Please, stop." He paced back and forth. I could see the veins in his neck and arms pulsing. "Fucking, Jared? Ais, what the fuck? He was a piece of shit back then, and even now. He has tried to steal everything from me my entire life, and you just gave him what is mine without hesitation? Fuck," he growled before stepping inches from my face, ready to kill me for hurting him.

I closed my eyes as I waited for the blow to smash my face in. I had never been hit by him before, but for this, I probably deserved it.

"Ais," he exhaled heavily before sniffling. His hand slowly caressed my cheek before it was gone, and I heard the rattle of keys as the door slammed, making me open my eyes to an empty apartment.

I knew when I told him he would probably leave. I had meant it when I told him to. Only because I knew that once he knew the truth, he would never talk to me again, and I had just recently begun to get used to him being around, even enjoying it. But he did exactly what I had expected, and now a pit in my stomach grew as I knew that I would never hear from him again. I should probably head back to Wisconsin and take a break from my past, present, and future.

I let the tears flow as I grabbed the bottle of wine and the bubble bath from the grocery bag and headed to the bathroom. Filling the tub with steaming water and undressing, letting my broken self sink under the water and bubbles, I let the never-ending tears finally flow. *Are you happy now, Ais? You finally pushed him away from your toxic self, and now you can be the lonely self-destructive woman that you are.* I stared up from under the water and nodded as I accepted my fate from here on out. I slid back up and sucked in a deep breath before screaming at the top of my lungs, hoping that would help take the stress out of me. I popped the cork off the bottle and chugged it. Today had just started to make me feel that my life could be good, and instead, another crazy spiral began.

Chapter 9
One Mistake

My bed felt too big and lonely as the wine consumed me, and the room began to spin. I searched for my phone and dialed Jameson's number, hoping to at least get his voicemail to say something. Anything. But I had no words left besides how sorry I was. But those words weren't going to be enough. Jameson would be gone from my life forever. He would never forgive me for any of this.

At least I felt better getting the weight off my shoulders. Jared, on the other hand, would be halfway out of New York by now. I half smiled at the thought of never seeing that manipulating liar ever again. The memories flowed back in as I remembered finding out the next day that Jameson was never seeing the colleague at all, and instead, they were just using each other for gain with the paparazzi. A legit business move. Jameson hadn't moved on from me at all at that point. That was when I started to distance myself from him and let my own pact be true for me too. I needed a fresh start and a new path after so much damage, knowing that I had a secret that I did not want to share.

I had stayed in Wisconsin long enough to finish college and get my degree in writing and journalism, leading me to New York to a few small bookshops before Mark My Words offered me Sarah's assistant job before promoting me to editor. I had succeeded this far by myself. I didn't need anyone's help. I knew what the hell I was doing, and I was good at my job. I could feel the tears coming back as the spinning room became a tornado. I decided it was time to go to sleep in my lonely bed that would be empty for a long time now. I had hoped for a dreamless night, but my spiraling mind had other plans.

I just needed to grab the box from Jameson's room and get the hell out of there. After the past week in the hospital for the miscarriage and my concussion, and then another week moping at home, I just needed a fresh start. Moving out of this small town would help. Everything here reminds me of him. I can't even walk down the street without having memories flood me, and now he's moved on. We had too much history here, and the minute he left, my world crumbled. I couldn't be here without him anymore. It was time.

I drove up to his place and held myself together as I quickly knocked on his parents' door, hoping someone would be home so that I wouldn't have to get the courage to come back here tomorrow. I just needed my stuff so that I could leave this town for good. Jameson was moving on, so I should too. It was honestly what was best for him, and I needed to accept that. And who knew if I'd ever make it far enough away from this town for him to even find me again. I hoped not.

The door creaked open, and his brother answered shirtless. My eyes went to his overworked abs and built frame, and I caught myself staring. His jeans were hanging lower than his hips as he flexed against the doorway, smirking.

"Oh, hi, Jared. I just need to grab some things from Jameson's room." I looked away quickly and tried to distract myself, but I could feel his eyes burning through me.

"Sure, yeah. Come on in." He smiled and moved past the door, letting me pass him.

He followed me into Jameson's room and watched as I packed the last few things into the box that I had left over there.

"So, you two are for sure done, huh?" he asked, biting his lower lip.

"It seems so." My hand had moved to my stomach out of habit, no longer growing the baby that was inside me.

Jared's eyes followed my hand as his eyes grew, and the small bulge that was still present but not noticeably enough for anyone to notice with the slightly baggier shirts I had been wearing.

He grabbed a toothpick off of his brother's dresser and put it between his teeth. I watched as his jaw tightened on the tiny piece of wood, making his smirk grow.

"You got something to tell me?" he pointed back to my stomach. I adjusted my shirt and crossed my arms, shaking my head.

"Huh, your secret is safe with me." He smiled and stepped closer toward the bed. "I take it that you saw the magazine cover too? Jameson called the other day and has been slaying women out there left and right. A new whore every night. It's disgusting really. I guess it's true what they say about small town boys. Bring them to a big city to become a man." He laughed and shrugged. "Pity, really. He had you."

I looked up and just stared at him, confused. "He never said anything to me about other women."

"Well, why would he? I'm his brother, we share pussy stories. I know all about yours. I would've treated you better, though," he said, as he walked past me and sat on the bed, leaning against the wall.

"Fuck off," I snapped back, the hormones inside me still raging. Pissed that I lost Jameson and our baby, which could have been a brighter future. Pissed that he was seeing other women, even though I knew that was our pact. I just didn't think it would happen that soon. Especially when I was going through so much alone. But how would Jameson know? I kept it a secret to not distract him. Stupid and young. Damn it. I ruined us. Not Jameson, me.

Jared laughed, "Wow, Ais I thought we were friends. That wasn't nice."

"I'm sorry," I said, ashamed. I sat down next to him. "I just thought that–"

"That he wouldn't forget about you? Yeah, I thought the same about me. He's too busy being famous and successful now. We are scum to him." He laced his hands behind his head and let his abs flex. I stared at him and studied his features. Being Jameson's brother, only eleven months younger than him and having a few similar features, they shared the same eyes and lips. Everything else was completely different. Jared did have a nice body, though. I caught myself distracted by his core.

He laughed as he scratched his muscles. "You don't have to look away."

"Ew, Jared, stop it," I declared before standing up and packing the rest of my things.

Jared stood up and helped pack the rest of my stuff, letting his hand rest on mine after putting the last thing into the box and sealing it.

"That's everything?" he asked.

I nodded.

"You don't have to leave yet. Just stay, you can talk to me." He smiled as he reached for his back pocket. "Here, check this out." He handed me his phone with a list of places that Jameson had already or was going to invest in.

I grimaced as I saw the success. Then, I felt guilty and waited for the tears to spill over.

"Successful shithead. I'm proud of him, but–" he inhaled slowly and shook his head as he exhaled. "Ais, I'm sorry my brother is an ass. I never would've hurt

you the way he did." He gently moved the hair out of my face and stopped the tears as they started to fall down my cheeks. His touch made me nervous, but I was so angry, and I just wanted to feel something. The spark that it gave me even out of anger made something ignite inside me. Maybe because of my heart being broken, the physical touch made something inside me blush. And for the first time in the last few weeks, I was happy to feel anything again. I felt my cheeks turn red at the intimacy. Jared watched closely as he lifted his other hand and held my face between his hands. "Let me fix your heart. Let me take care of you."

Every fiber inside my being told me to run, told me to get away from him. But my heart was so broken, and I just wanted to feel anything, and right then, anything seemed better than feeling nothing. He lifted my chin up as his lips came down onto mine. His tongue slipped between my lips, my mouth moving in sync with his. My body was moving faster than my brain could. For the first time in weeks, I felt something. And that's all I want right now. I wanted to heal and move on. Fuck Jameson. He's moved on. He will never be back for me. I am nothing to him. Fuck it. Fuck him. Fuck.

I could feel something inside me ignite and didn't give a fuck about anything anymore. This was my life, and I was never going to let another man hold my heart the way I let Jameson. He held my whole future and then threw it away when he decided to become a manwhore in New York. Fuck him.

Tonight was a new me. A me that wouldn't be hurt like this again. Emotions were just a switch, and this was one that I needed to turn off. I could be happy too. I just needed to stop feeling right now and not think about the future. Just act in the moment. Fuck you, Jameson.

I grabbed Jared's face and pulled him fiercely into me, letting him lay me back on Jameson's bed and undress me. He started off slowly while he took my bra off and brought his mouth to my nipples, biting them gently and exploring my entire body as I let him pull my jeans down.

Fuck you, Jameson.

Jared looked up and smirked, "You're sure?"

I leaned up on my elbows and took my thong off, while pushing Jared's face down and making him shut his mouth and give me the orgasm I needed. The amount of pleasure he was fulfilling was supposed to be filling the void I was feeling. But nothing was happening. I tried to focus on myself and get to an orgasm, but something deep inside me was screaming for me to stop this. But I was pissed. Fuck you, Jameson.

He leaned over and grabbed a condom, tearing the wrapper and readying himself before thrusting hard inside me. I winced at the roughness of it, without being wet enough for him. I had never had that problem with his brother. Just having Jameson's tongue wrestling with mine could get me ready. He thrusted again as he pulled me closer to him. I wanted it to feel good. I wanted it to fill the void that I needed him to, but it wasn't, and he was not a gentle lover.

"You good?" he groaned.

I nodded as he grabbed me and flipped me over, thrusting his dick into me again. Knowing that I asked him to do this for me, I gripped the blanket tighter.

Fuck you, Jameson.

Jared panted faster as each thrust got deeper and deeper. His entire body laid on top of me as he finished into the condom, holding me against his sweating body to prolong the minutes that we were together. He turned me around and kissed my neck slowly, then my torso, which made me realize that he knew exactly what secret I had been holding from his brother all along. He chuckled softly. "Mmm, I win."

He sat back up, pushing me back down onto the bed. Then, he started to clean himself up and tossed the towel back to me. I looked up at him, confused.

"You win?" I asked, catching my breath. "What the fuck does that mean?"

He laughed as he walked toward the door.

"Jared," I choked.

"My brother had everything. But now I've had you, willingly." He smirked and winked as he walked out of the room, leaving me alone in my thoughts.

I sat back on the bed, dressing myself as I felt disgusted with my own actions. What have I done? My phone rang, which made me jump. Jameson's name went across the screen, and I instantly felt shame and anger. I stood up, grabbed the box of stuff and headed out the door.

"Come over anytime, Ais." Jared yelled, as I stormed past him.

I hopped into my car and bawled the entire ride home, ignoring each phone call from Jameson. Unsure how that conversation would go.

Voicemail, 1 New Message.

Shit.

I grabbed my phone and listened while I was parked in front of my house, letting the tears dry before I walked inside.

"Hey, Ais. I'm sorry I haven't called lately. I have been working late hours, and finally, it has paid off. Say hello to the newest New York investor who just got one of the largest partners in the US to give me a shot. One year from today, and I will own half of New York, just wait and see. Today has been the best day of my life. The only thing missing from it is you. I would do anything to have you here with me right now. But I know that we made a pact. I have not, and will not, date anyone yet. Not until you tell me we are done. I cannot see my life without you yet, and I hope you stick with me through my successes because they are just as much yours too. I would not be here if it wasn't for you forcing me to leave. I am building our future out here, and I hope that you will one day join me in it. I love you, baby. Always have, always will."

I threw my phone across the dashboard and watched as the screen shattered along with my heart. Jared was a fucking manipulating liar. He used me to get back at Jameson. The fucking bastard.

"Oh. My. God," I screamed as I felt my world crumble.

Shattered, I walked inside and decided I was breaking free from these memories. My future would be bright. I just needed a fresh start and to let it all go. Including Jameson.

Chapter 10
Imposter Syndrome

I woke up with a pounding headache. Wine, tears, and regrets were not a good combo along with a memory I tried to bury deep into its grave. A few weeks ago, when Jameson showed up at the bar, celebrating yet another success, I was there having a drink as I did every year on that day. It had been a tradition ever since Jared made me feel small, and I decided I would never let anyone make me feel so used again, that the only day I would celebrate would be the day I decided to let myself be reborn. The day I let the Aisling Lux that I was today start fresh down a better path.

Of course, out of all days, the universe decided to intertwine Jameson's spath with mine yet again. It was a stupid twist of fate that now forced the secret out and brought me down into a spiral of the past again, just as my life was starting to see the light again. I checked my phone and was surprised but relieved when there wasn't anything on it. No phone calls, no voicemails, no messages. Nothing.

I debated on texting Jameson. Then, I closed it. He would no longer want to talk to me, and I didn't blame him. I needed to let him go, it's what I had intended in the first place. He deserved better. Here he was, in New York a decade ago, planning a future for us while I was home fucking his brother. I was an idiot. I still had regrets, but I couldn't let it take over my future. I jumped up and got ready for work. If my job was still there, or if my "boss" sold the company back overnight… I grimaced at the thought of the building being burned down by karma to spite me. Almost had it all and then boom, burn bitch.

My heels were waiting for me by the table where the dinner never came out of the bag. I grabbed the bag to walk it to the trash when I felt something poke me from inside it. I opened it to see a sealed envelope on top of the carryout container. I stood back, debating on if this should be burned or opened. It would surely be something sweet, and I wasn't prepared to cry anymore today. I tossed it on the table and decided to read it later tonight after I kicked ass at work. I would stop and grab something stronger to drink for that envelope.

Slipping my heels on and grabbing my phone, I headed to the door to leave. Staring behind me at the table, where a few nights ago one of my favorite nights happened, it was now the saddest spot where I broke his heart. I made a mental note to burn the damn table, and who knows maybe I'd burn the letter with it. I slammed the door and headed to my company.

Sarah walked into my office behind me before I could even sit down. "Miss Aisling, um. Marleigh is here. She wants to see you."

I stopped walking and turned around, shocked. "Did she say what for?"

Sarah shook her head, "No, ma'am."

"Shit. Okay, give me two minutes and let her in please."

Sarah nodded and walked back out.

I quickly cleared my desk and made it look professional before wishing her manuscript was sitting in the center. I grimaced when I thought about her visit today, what this could mean if she asked for the script and it wasn't here. I looked up and smiled as Marleigh walked into my office, smiling from ear to ear.

"Oh my, this office suits you. Devon was an asshole anyway. I only came to this company for you. Jameson had talked you up so much that I knew I had to have you." She winked and took a seat without waiting.

"It's so nice to see you. What can I help you with?" I asked.

"Actually," she hesitated before seeming nervous. "Would you mind taking a break from your work and coming out for breakfast with me?"

I was shocked at her question and politely raised my eyebrow. "Me? I mean–"

"Listen, I am having the worst imposter syndrome about my book, and I just need my editor to be my friend for a bit and give it to me straight. Is it garbage?

Should I start over at page one? Should I burn the whole thing?"

My jaw dropped as the number one New York best seller was freaking out in my office and asking for me to hype her up. *Like what?* "Marleigh, your book is amazing, and I have read it nearly a hundred times, line for line. Literally."

"Stop it, you're just being nice."

Best friend girl mode kicked in with this early forties woman, and I decided she needed a distraction as badly as me. "That's it. Let's go."

I lifted her arm and we walked out of the building arm in arm and headed for the nearest bar. "We need mimosas or tequila flights," I laughed, but I hadn't decided which would be best for me yet.

Marleigh had a way with words and being an author was definitely the path she was born for. The hours passed as she confided in me about her growing career, twisted love life, and the fame game. We were able to get our own table on the rooftop of the closest bar, due to Marleigh signing two copies of her book for the bartender's wife, and he let the drinks come ever since to our private table.

"Do you ever regret it?" she asked me.

I looked at her confused. Most of our conversations had been about her today, and I had not mentioned anything about Jameson.

"I'm sorry, regret what?"

"Don't you ever regret leaving Wisconsin? You know, small town life with less chaos?"

I laughed, if only she knew the amount of chaos that just followed me, no matter where I went. Jameson's sad eyes came to mind when I thought about how in love we were back home, and now how I just shattered him.

"Aisling, are you okay?" Marleigh leaned closer to me and patted my leg. "Did I say something?"

"Not at all. I do miss the small town, but really, once Jameson left, it didn't feel like home anymore." I answered truthfully, surprising myself with pure honesty.

Marleigh's eyes met mine, and she smiled. "So, why are you two not an item yet?"

I inhaled slowly and shook my head. "It's complicated."

Marleigh laughed, "Everything is complicated, that's life. If life was always easy, we would get bored, wouldn't we?"

I nodded and smiled back at her.

"Besides, the true question is can he love you at your worst?" she pointed her finger at me as if teaching me a lesson that I didn't want to learn. "If he can do that, then it's true love and eventually will work itself out."

I laughed while taking another shot of tequila. "That's the famous line from your manuscript, you can't use that on me. I have read those lines hundreds of times."

She laughed, "Well, then, you know it's true. I only write what matters."

I looked back at her, catching my breath. "Your writing is perfect. Imposter syndrome is no more. Promise me that you won't doubt yourself anymore because the world loves your work."

Marleigh looked back at me and nodded. "Thank you. Not just for the compliment, but actually spending time with me. Sometimes I get lonely in this big city, and I both love and hate it."

I smiled as I understood that more than anything. The loneliness I felt for the last decade while burying myself in my work was what I wanted to feel, as if I had accomplished my goals.

Marleigh stood and did a quick wobble to steady herself. "I think it's time for me to get a taxi home. My couch and sweatpants are calling my name. Plus, I have a tub of mint chocolate chip ice cream waiting for me." We laughed as we headed for the stairs. She must not drink a lot, or my tolerance was getting too high because I felt pretty good still. I decided that I had work to do back at the office. I would probably be the only one left in the building, but that would be even better. I could use some alone time.

"Thank you, Marleigh," I said, as I hugged her tight before she stepped into her cab, winking.

"Go get that man of yours." She smiled as she waved back at me.

I took a deep breath and started to head back toward the office. I stared at the sign above the door before stepping into my company and felt the guilt come back as I knew I did not earn this place, at least not yet. I stepped into my office and was shocked when

I saw a familiar stack of papers on my desk. I walked closer and froze when I saw my initials in the top corner. It was Marleigh's manuscript with a post-it on it.

It's all yours. Thank you for the offer. Maybe for the next book. – Lena

I walked behind the desk and sat down in my chair and spun happily around in circles like a child would do.

"Yes!" I yelled excitedly. I flipped the book open to where I had left off and got to work. Thinking of the time just spent with Marleigh sparked an idea for me. Getting to know each author before publishing felt right. Marleigh felt like a friend now and not just a business partner. After another hour had passed, I smiled as my highlighter finished the last edit for the manuscript.

One hour. That was all I had needed before the big plan to sabotage me had occurred. I had only brought the manuscript with me that night to finish it. I had been so excited and decided to go out that night and celebrate. Then, Jameson was there.

I grabbed my phone and decided to call him. I just needed to hear his voice. Hear that he was okay. Just hear him breathing. I dialed his number and hung up after the first ring.

Stupid.

He doesn't want to hear from me. He probably wished I were dead after that betrayal. I set my phone back down and let my hands shake nervously until I could catch my breath.

He doesn't want you anymore.

I sniffled and nodded to myself before my phone rang, making me jump at the unexpected callback.

Jameson's name appeared on the screen. I debated for two rings whether I was supposed to answer it or let it go to voicemail.

I held my breath as I accepted the call.

"Ais?"

Letting my breath out, "Yes, hey."

"Where are you?"

I hesitated. "I'm just finishing up at work."

"Thought so. Stay there."

I felt nervous all of a sudden, and my stomach started to turn as the line disconnected.

I jumped up and quickly looked in the mirror hanging on the wall, pinching my cheeks to help the blood flow back to my face. I quickly tried to brighten my eyes by adding concealer under my lashes. I tussled my hair and readjusted my skirt, trying to feel confident in this unplanned meeting that was surely going to be another disaster.

I dimmed the lights in the office so that he couldn't watch me cry when he decided to leave me for good. I leaned up against my desk, arms crossed before realizing that looked defensive and bitchy. I changed positions to have my arms leaning back on the table and then readjusted again when that seemed too seductive. I heard the elevator door open and knew he was only steps away. I stood awkwardly as he walked through my door.

"Jameson," I whispered, as he closed the space between us.

Chapter 11
Please Don't Hate Me Forever

Jameson was standing in front of me, inching our way back against the desk. I breathed heavily, unsure of what was going to happen next. I watched carefully as his fist came up and slammed down on the desk next to me, making me flinch.

I looked up at his face and gasped when I saw the broken lip and bruised cheekbone. I quickly grabbed his face and steadied him. "Jameson, what happened?"

He slammed his other fist down and leaned his head into my chest, breathing heavily. I rubbed his head and tried to comfort him, in his torment that I had caused.

"I'm so sorry. I never meant to hurt you." I whispered.

His fists relaxed and met the small of my back pulling me in tighter to him. His head was still leaning against me, hiding his emotions from me. I pulled his head back and tried to see his face, but he leaned harder against me.

"I never knew," he finally said. "You went through everything alone." He squeezed me tighter as he lifted me onto my desk and spread my legs to stand between them. His rollercoaster of emotions was finally meeting my eyes.

"I never told you, it was my fault." I rubbed the bruise that was forming on his cheekbone, afraid to ask where it came from. I felt that I already knew the answer, but I needed to hear it from him. "What happened?"

His hand covered mine as it cradled his face. "Don't worry about it."

I frowned as I watched his expression change into a half smile.

"I was waiting outside your apartment. I thought you would've been home by now."

I half smiled back at him. "I had to finish the manuscript," I said proudly.

He looked past my body on the oversized desk and saw the papers sitting behind me. "You got it back."

I nodded, "And it's finished."

He lifted me up and spun me around. The tequila showed its face again with the spinning. And I laughed, making him stop. "Never doubted you." He looked up to me, in his arms still, as he walked me back to the desk.

"You only bought the whole company thinking that I would fail." I laughed.

He snorted, "Not why I bought it." He moved my hair out of my face as he set me back down on the desk. My legs automatically wrapped around his torso without thinking. Muscle memory was harder to retrain than the mental habits. He held his hands underneath my lifted legs and smirked.

"Jameson, what happened to your face?" I asked, bringing back reality.

"Don't ask. It's done."

Instantly, my mind went to Jared, and I knew that he had found his brother. Now how alive he was was the real question.

"You don't hate me?" I whispered, leaning back and waiting for his answer.

He scoffed before pulling me closer to him. "Hate you? My brother manipulated you to get back at me. How is that your fault?"

"Well, I hate to admit it, but I didn't stop him, either."

Jameson's eyes locked with mine. "You are mine. Do you understand me?"

I felt the blood rush to my cheeks as he said it.

"I will not share you," he growled. "Especially not with him."

My body shivered at the words, and I couldn't decide if the weight of those words was sexy, or if they scared me.

"So, you're not leaving me?" I bit my lower lip and waited for the answer I hoped was true.

"Never again."

I pulled him harder against me and let his lips crush into mine with a fierceness of never letting go. His hips moved with mine as our bodies grinded between us, letting the elephant that had been in between us for a decade finally explode, knowing we could get past it all. It was a second chance, and I sure as hell wasn't messing this up again.

He lifted my shirt over my head before laying me back on the desk where work needed to be done, but right now it could all wait. He lifted my skirt and lowered his head between my legs, making me shiver with excitement. The heat made my blood flow faster as his lips met mine. He knew exactly what he was doing. I moaned as his tongue slipped inside me and moved faster, so much need. My lower back arched as the pleasure became too intense to lay still.

"Okay, okay," I whispered, pulling his head back up to mine. Panting against his body, I was wet and ready for more. He grabbed my bra and ripped it off, grabbing my breasts in his hands as his tongue slipped into my mouth. I sucked on it hard as he groaned.

"You. Are. Mine." He groaned louder while unbuttoning his pants.

I nodded while trying to catch my breath. It was exactly what I wanted. I wanted him, all of him, for me, only me, *forever*. Grabbing his face, I kissed him, less urgently and more sweet to savor this moment with him as a sober moment, and not a late night fuck.

"I'm yours, baby," I whispered into his ear.

He locked eyes with me and smiled before slowly entering me, moving back and forth without looking away. My hand held tight behind his head, letting the orgasm reach and continue, holding his gaze and letting all of the last decade disappear and become a part of our past. Letting us have a future. His hips thrusted fast, matching our breathing, pulling me closer into him. We reached our climax together and panted while laying on top of the oversized desk that would now never allow me to get work done again without fantasizing about his body on top of it.

"I love you," I whispered.

"I love you more, Ais." He kissed my neck and held me close for a little while longer.

Tonight's encounter was unexpected and even though he would not tell me about fighting his demons. He also insisted on staying while I locked up and driving me home. Something inside me told me that he did not want to be alone tonight. The fight between him and Jared must've been more of a mindfuck than he was letting in on. But I didn't dare to bring up his name again after everything that happened.

I locked the last door as Jameson wrapped his arm around my shoulders and led me to his parked car.

"I went to the gym and boxed with Cameron," he said once we were in the car.

"Oh," was all I could say, because honestly, I was shocked that it wasn't a brawl with Jared. Also, Cameron was such a nice guy that I felt guilty that the two of them would spar together.

He looked over from the driver seat and smirked. "I didn't like him having his hands on you the other night. Plus, he's my gym buddy. It was bound to happen."

I sat quietly, replaying the other night with Cameron. "Did he say anything about me?"

"Well, that's why I got this." He pointed to his cheekbone and smirked. "I needed him to know that you were mine."

My jaw dropped. "So, you hit him? Oh my god. Jameson, he's such a nice guy, why wou–."

He laughed. "I'm kidding. We spar at the gym all the time. I did tell him, however, that my intentions were to win you back and then we had a good laugh, and he took an unfair shot." He pointed to his face. "You should see his."

I rolled my eyes. "Cameron is nice."

"He would never be good enough for you."

"And you are?" I snapped back with a smirk, almost wanting to swallow my sarcasm the minute I said it. Because truthfully, he really did deserve better.

He parked the car and turned to face me. "Of course not." He frowned before jumping out of the car and running to open my door. "But I am not the worst thing, either."

I smirked and stepped out of the car, refusing his hand and doing it myself. "Will you stay the night?" I figured it was best to ask while I still had my courage.

He nodded as we walked to the entrance of my apartment, letting things go and starting fresh.

Chapter 12
Late Nights and Forever Talks

It had to be midnight, as we had just laid in bed having pillow talk for the last few hours about nothing and everything. I hadn't dared to bring up Jared's name yet, but it would have to be dealt with eventually. Jared wasn't going to stop. We both knew it. Over the decade, he had continued to find me and obsess over me, or really, obsess over trying to get under my skin and his brother's every chance he could.

Jameson's dark hair was messy and falling on his forehead in such a casual way that it made him seem younger than we were. It reminded me of who we were before our lives changed. The urge to mess with his hair came over me, and I tousled it between my fingers, smiling as his happiness overwhelmed me.

"Are you happy in New York?" he asked me.

I contemplated the question and debated about the word, happy. Was I?

"I am content with where I am."

"Not happy?" his eyebrows furrowed as he sat up on his elbow.

I sucked in a breath and chose my words carefully. "I am still learning how to be happy. I have spent so many years pleasing everyone else and trying to get ahead that I didn't really know my own worth and that my own happiness mattered. If that makes sense?"

He nodded and seemed to frown. "Me too."

I sat up on my elbow, mimicking him, "No, not the great Jameson Tonic, mathematical genius, number one eligible bachelor, and millionaire in New York, unhappy?" I giggled as I pushed his shoulder over, making his body tip as he laid on his back. Jumping on top of him, I straddled his torso. "The man who has it all and still isn't smiling." I tickled his sides and watched as his body tensed as he tried to hold in his laughter.

He grabbed my wrists and shook his head. "I might be a little happy." He smirked and pulled me down onto him, holding me tight.

I caught my breath and laid against him, letting his arms wrap around me as I fit perfectly to him.

"Where would you like to go?" he whispered softly into my ear.

"Nowhere right now." I pulled his arms tighter against me, afraid that he was getting ready to leave me alone in this bed.

He laughed. "I mean, if you were to leave New York, where would you want to go?"

I thought of Wisconsin and the small town that we came from. I did miss the four seasons there, watching the leaves change colors instead of tall buildings blocking the view, and the quietness of it, but then again, when things were too quiet, my brain went into overthinking mode. That was never good, either.

"I think I like it here. I like that every night can be different, it doesn't have to be, but I have the option to do so many things here. Back home, we just had one diner and one bar, and half the time, one would be closed so the other would get the business." We laughed. "I like the chaos here. I think it's been better the last few weeks."

"Because of me?"

I shoved away from him and looked back at him, sarcastically, "Ew, no."

He laughed and pulled me in closer against him again. "Stop pulling away," he said, his voice becoming hoarse as sleep was starting to consume him. I relaxed my body as he kissed my shoulder.

"Yes, because of you."

I could hear his breathing become even and steady, and I knew he was sleeping. I smiled to myself at the happiness I felt right now. I accomplished things that I had only dreamed of over the years, all in the past few months. Jameson helped me along with the company part, but I truly believed that Marleigh's book was going to bring me to the top regardless. So even though he helped, I was still going to keep some of the credit for my hard work.

At some point, I had fallen asleep and had a dreamless night. My body and mind needed the peace, as I woke up feeling much more rested. I turned around to see Jameson still sleeping next to me. I kissed his forehead and snuck out from under his arm to head to the kitchen. I reached the doorway and turned to see him still sleeping, peacefully.

I headed to the kitchen and started to brew some coffee and searched the fridge for anything to make for breakfast, frowning as I realized I didn't have anything to make him. "Damn it."

"Swearing so early in the morning?" he asked, while walking up behind me and kissing my neck. He grabbed two mugs to fill.

"Surprised you stayed," I said, lifting my head up from the empty fridge.

"You asked me to." He smiled as he added my two sugars with vanilla and caramel creamer to my mug. Then reached for the cinnamon.

"Huh, you remember?" I asked, slightly embarrassed.

He smiled. "Of course. Now I think it's only fair if you let me properly take you out to breakfast. It doesn't have to be a date, but a charity to feed that starving stomach of yours." He smiled and waited.

I rolled my eyes and nodded. "Only because I am hungry." I grabbed my coffee filled mug and headed toward the bathroom. "Give me twenty minutes."

He leaned back in the chair and stretched.

He drove us deeper into the city for New York's top rated Belgium waffles. Jameson insisted on paying for breakfast. I rolled my eyes, knowing that money did not matter to him, but my pride still was intact, and today's meal was on me. He could pay the next time if he was serious about sticking around.

The waitress came and left, and while we waited for the food, I decided it was time to ask.

"I know you don't want to talk about it, but does your brother know I told you?" I regretted it the minute I asked.

He looked up, eyebrow raised. "Why do you care?"

I shifted in my seat, "He…" I froze as Lena walked through the door alone and waited to see who her company was. I scanned the room for Jared and realized he was nowhere to be seen. Then, I saw another woman walk in after Lena, smiling and joining her. I exhaled the breath I didn't know I was holding and brought myself back to reality. But Jameson was already following my gaze, then stood up and walked over to Lena near the entrance. I sat quietly, trying to hear his conversation with her, but the place was too damn loud with hungover teenagers and whiny college girls who were definitely here on daddy's money.

Jameson met me back at the table, frustrated. "Sorry, you were saying?"

I watched as Lena took her table with her friend, "He scares me."

His jaw hardened as I said the words. I could see his temper exploding inside of him. The thought of Jared touching me, let alone hurting me, would certainly make Jameson want to kill him. I leaned over the table and reached for his hand, rubbing it gently and bringing his thoughts back to this very moment.

"Hey, it's fine," I said.

"It's definitely not fine, but it will be once I find the fucker."

And there it was. He was furious, but was trying to keep his temper in control so that he didn't do anything he would regret down the road or that could ruin his career. A brawl with his brother on the front page could easily have some companies wanting to pull away from him and find a new investor if they believed him to be dangerous or going off the deep end. Which seemed to be exactly what Jared had been trying to do.

Our waitress walked up with our plates as he said it, and she took a step back, shocked.

"Not you." I smiled and shook my head. She nodded and set the plates down.

"Can I get you two anything else?" she asked, and I shook my head quickly.

"We're fine, thank you."

She left and let us be.

"My brother has been hell bent on revenge since the day I left him back home. He has hated me for leaving. For a decade, he has tried everything to get under my skin. But for good reason, he has left that detail out of his mouth, and now I know why."

I wasn't following him.

"He finally got what he wanted, but instead of hurting me, he hurt himself by falling for someone who doesn't want him back."

I swallowed hard remembering that night. Jared's smile as he walked away from me was not one of wanting me. He wanted to destroy his brother.

"Do you think he left New York?" I asked, hoping that he had.

"Lena said she broke it off with him last night, and he was furious. She has no idea where he went afterwards."

I looked around the restaurant and scanned for him again.

"You don't think he would try anything stupid, do you?"

"What, like come after me or something? No, he's jealous, but he's still my brother. Blood is thicker than revenge."

I had a bad feeling about this, but kept my mouth closed for now. Picking up my fork, I dug into the whipped cream and strawberries, filling my belly with deliciousness. Top rated, and for good reason. These were amazing.

"What's on the agenda for today?" I asked in between spoonfuls.

He looked up and laughed. "You're not sick of me yet?"

I laughed, covering my mouth full of food, and swallowed quickly. "Not yet, ask me again next week."

"So, you want me around for another week? That's good progress, coming from the woman who has pushed me away for a decade. Miss 'you should probably leave.'" He smirked.

I put my fork down and grabbed my coffee, slowly sipping on it, watching him from behind the mug. "I mentally prepared myself years ago that you were never going to speak to me again. So, to have you still wanting to be near me and sharing delicious waffles with me is better progress than I ever expected."

"Ais, I never would've left Wisconsin had I known–"

"Stop. That is exactly why I didn't tell you right away, and by the time I was going to, I lost her, and then I lost myself."

He shook his head in anger. "I should've been there."

I thought he was angry with me, but instead, he was beating himself up about it. I shook my head. We both wanted to blame ourselves about the past.

He grabbed my hand, "We're starting over."

I furrowed my brows and pointed to the waffles. "I think breakfast is a good start."

"I'm sorry I wasn't there for you." He looked up with sincere eyes.

Waving him off, I moved on. "I'm sorry I didn't tell you sooner. We were just so young." I inhaled sharply and let it out. "If we can love each other at our worst, then eventually, it will work itself out." I smiled, knowing that Marleigh's words came in handy. "Can we just agree that the past happened and doesn't have to define our future?"

He smiled and nodded. "Okay."

"Okay." I smiled back at him.
"Let's get out of here."

Chapter 13
Another Day, Another Drama

The weekend was going by fast. Jameson was called into work with some kind of building fire that had started, and he had to deal with the insurance company. He called for a taxi and paid for the man to take me home, knowing that we had to go in opposite directions. Before leaving, he pulled me in for a kiss in front of the many onlookers. Lifting the small of my back, he pulled me up into his embrace as a paparazzi was walking into the restaurant and noticed who he was before snapping a picture. He set me down and smirked. "Now New York will know you are mine." Smiling, he insisted that I get home and relax, and he would meet me later if I would allow him to.

I reached my apartment and stepped out of the taxi, thanking him. Shocked, I saw Cameron standing outside my building.

"I just needed to tell you myself," he said as he walked toward me. "Had I known that Jameson was involved with you–"

I covered his mouth, not wanting any more drama for today. "Cameron, you are beyond nice and deserve only the best." I could feel his lips curl into a smile as I lowered my hand. "Jameson and I have history, and it seems like we might actually have a future too." I smiled at the thought. "You know what, if you're free right now, then come upstairs. It's kind of a long story."

My thoughts went to Sarah right away. She deserved someone as nice as Cameron, and I wanted to mention it to him.

He hesitated for a minute, and when he turned his head, I saw the shiner around his eye. "Oh, the right hook?" I asked. And he laughed, nodding.

"He's my friend. This was for fun," he said, pointing.

My eyes bulged at the word fun. I'd hate to see anything less than fun.

We walked up to my apartment and froze when I saw my door partially opened. Cameron crossed his arm in front of me, stopping me.

"Did you leave that open?" he whispered, and I shook my head.

He pushed me behind him and slowly opened the door to my apartment, stepping inside. I walked in behind him and scanned the empty apartment. Relief washed over me. I walked toward my bedroom as he checked the guest room. I froze when I saw the envelope opened and a letter laying on my bed. I went to reach for it, but my body was forced against the wall, my mouth covered as his voice whispered in my ear.

"You fucking bitch, you told him." He took my head and slammed it against the wall, then tossed me onto the bed, pinning me down as I tried to squirm out of his grasp. My head was pounding.

"Get off me," I screamed, as my face burned from the bruise instantly forming on my face. I was lucky to not have been knocked out. Jared's fist came down toward me, but Cameron flew across the room, leveling Jared's body to the ground and landing a hit to his face. Jared pushed himself up, sending Cameron back against the wall, knocking the wind out of him. He got up and kicked Cameron in the ribs. *Fuck.* I jumped up and tried to get between them, only to be struck across the face by Jared's fist. My mouth burned, blood trickling down my chin.

Jared and Cameron froze and stared at me, the room closing in on itself around me. My legs buckled from underneath me. My eyes stayed open, but my body felt like it was in shock as I watched Cameron try to move past Jared to reach me, only to see Jared throw a right hook, matching his brother's and bringing Cameron down to my level while Jared ran out of the apartment.

Cameron slid closer to me and lifted me onto his lap, pulling his phone from his pocket before the room finally went dark.

Jared's voice screamed to me through the door of my apartment. I sat against the cold door and waited for him to leave. He never should've found where I lived. I ran from him two years ago and have tried to avoid every phone call and encounter possible since.

"You need to leave, or I will call the police, Jared."

He laughed and pounded on the door, "Let me in."

"Go, now," I screamed. "Just leave me alone."

The pounding stopped. I could hear his body slide against the wood as he sat down in the hallway, leaning against the door. "Why do you push me away?"

"You used me."

"I love you."

I scoffed at the words and wanted to vomit. "No, you used me out of revenge for your brother. You need help, Jared."

He breathed heavily. "I just need you. You make me feel something."

"Jared, you need to leave. Please. You're drunk, and this isn't going to end well for either of us."

After two years of not seeing him, the universe was sick and brought us to the same bar together in New York. I thought I had left in time before he saw me, but he ended up following me home. And now, here we were. Only a door between us. I didn't want him any closer to me. After what he did to me, I didn't want to see him ever again. He used me, and part of me was glad that it happened because it finally made me realize my self-worth and leave the small town for good. But the bigger part of me was disgusted at myself for letting it happen.

"Jared, please just go."

I heard him stand up and sniffle. "I know I fucked up. It started as revenge, but I can't stop thinking about you. The more you push me away, the more I want you, Ais. Please just talk to me. You're my only friend."

I wanted to scream that our friendship ended when he took advantage of my brokenness, but with alcohol in his system, he became like his abusive father, and I didn't want to take any chances.

"Jared, please. Not tonight."

My eyes felt swollen when I opened them. The room was dim enough that it had to be night out. The city lights were the only thing shining through the blinds to the room. I sat up slowly and regretted it the minute I did, a wave of nausea crashing over me.

"Woah, no, no. You need to sit still. I'll call the nurses," Jameson's voice instructed.

I opened my eyes again and saw him sitting in the chair next to me, Cameron sleeping in the chair at the foot of the bed.

Jameson pushed the button for clinical help as he moved to sit on the bed next to me, careful not to squish me. His hand reached my face, making me flinch, not meaning to because he didn't scare me, but I was afraid that my mind was playing tricks on me. I wanted to be sure it was him and not Jared.

He froze and studied my expression. "Hey, it's me. The police are searching for my brother now."

I nodded and tried to sit up again, only this time I was able to. The nurses entered the room as Cameron woke up and stood up quickly. His face was full of concern and worry, and two shiners. He stood at the end of the bed with his arms crossed as we all waited for the results. I suddenly felt embarrassed at everyone fussing over me.

The doctor came in and checked my pupils with a flashlight, blinding me. "She will be alright, just a heavy hit, no concussion." He stared at Jameson and Cameron. "Who's with her?" Jameson nodded as he flicked his hand in the air. "And you know who did this to her?" The doctor studied his expression and waited. "Mr. Tonic, if you get caught up in an abusive scandal, then your reputation could be tainted."

"I would never lay a hand on a woman. The police are looking for him now." He nodded, irritated at the suggestion.

Cameron nodded, "I was there, it wasn't him, sir."

The doctor nodded, "I always have to ask questions. It's my job."

They agreed as he walked out of the room, leaving the nurse to mend my pain. She gave me some pain pills and water. "We will keep her overnight just to be sure," she said before leaving.

"I'm going to grab some coffee, do you two want anything?" Cameron asked.

We both shook our heads as he put his hands in his pockets and left the room.

"I thought I told you to have a relaxing night," Jameson said, as he stood next to me, pushing my hair out of my face.

"What? This isn't relaxing?" I pointed to the pain pills before cheers-ing the air and swallowing them whole.

He laughed, but I could see he was fighting the urge to break something.

"Hey," I grabbed his arm. "It's okay."

"None of this is okay." He seemed lost in thought. "I never should've brought you into any of this."

I huffed, "This isn't any of your fault. My past finally caught up with me."

"It's my past, none of this should involve you. He's gone off the deep end. I didn't want to believe it when others warned me of it. But now I know, Jared needs to be locked up. He's showing signs of manic bipolar again, and he needs help. None of this would've happened if I wouldn't have left him to fend for himself with our shithead dad. My mom warned me about it before she passed. She said he seemed irritable lately, and I left him alone."

I shook my head. "This is not your fault. Jared is a grown man and can take the blame himself. There are no excuses for what he's done. I'm just glad it's me here and not Lena. I warned her of his temper, and I'm just glad she did not have to see it."

Jameson's eyes glared as he stared out of the window at the city. "You're coming home with me tonight. I don't want you back in that apartment."

"That is my place, it's safe."

"If he can break into it, then it's obviously not." He exhaled slowly. "Stay with me for a few days while I hire someone to make it safer. Please." He wasn't asking but pleading.

I nodded and was thankful for the company but sad to be temporarily moved from my own place that I had worked hard on getting. "Okay."

"What was Cameron doing at your place?" he asked without making eye contact.

I laughed at his jealousy kicking in and decided to relieve him from his thoughts. "He came to apologize on your behalf for the date, so I figured I owed him an explanation."

He smirked and met my eyes.

"I was going to mention my assistant, Sarah, to him. She deserves a date with a good man."

"Playing matchmaker?" he raised an eyebrow.

I laughed. "I'm sick of seeing her deadbeat, soon to be ex coming around her. She needs to see that good men do exist."

"As do you." His eyes locked with mine as he leaned in and kissed my broken lip carefully.

The week had been quiet. Staying in his suite was a whole new experience. I couldn't believe the view he had in upstate New York. I stood, drinking tea while staring out at the city lights in awe. Borrowing his oversized t-shirts and going panty-less, since I had not been back home since the incident, he offered to buy me new garments, but I think he liked the easy access whenever he saw fit, as did I. While staying at his place, I had to admit that it felt like a whole new city. I didn't know if it was the place, or if it was because he was here with me.

He had still gone into work each day this week but made me promise to keep my phone near me for anything that I needed. He would send his female assistant on any errands for me, but I assured him that I was fine and that he couldn't make me into a prisoner here. I was fully capable of running my own errands to the store close by. I would not make my way back to the apartment until the place was secure for both his and my sake.

Jared had still not been found. The cops seemed to be taking their time finding him, which made me uneasy, but he would pay his own bail anyway. So, it would only be temporary security. I touched my face and felt the swelling starting to go down, which made me feel more like myself again, and for that, I was thankful for.

I decided to call Sarah and ask if she would bring the manuscript and my laptop to finish the uploads for Marleigh. My deadline was Monday, and I knew that I still wanted to make it work. She agreed and asked if I needed anything else. I smiled, asking if she could stop and grab my coffee on her way. Whether it was her new raise or just her being a concerned friend, I was happy I had her around. I gave her the address, and she gasped when she realized where I was staying.

"You lucky woman," she giggled. "Please, give me a tour, I've always wanted to see inside one of those places."

I laughed and agreed. If she would give Cameron a chance, she would realize he owns one very similar two blocks down from Jameson. I figured it was time to plant the seed for her.

"Hey, can you grab the coffee from the shop on the corner? It's–"

"Your favorite. I know." She laughed before disconnecting.

I looked at the clock and hoped that fate would do its job and have Cameron there getting his normal wake up call drink right about now. Each Thursday, he was there for our encounters, so I hoped he would still be. Once he saw Sarah, there would be no turning away from her.

I quickly got dressed into the pair of clothes that I had with me and walked around to pick up a little, not meaning to be nosey but also trying to keep myself useful as I waited. Straightening the magazines, I paused when I saw the female that triggered me to think that he had moved on years ago, on the front cover of most successful women this year. I wanted to glare at it, but then I realized that she meant no harm. They had teamed up to make themselves advance faster in their career. Just seeing her made me remember my bad night, though, and I decided to take her cover and place it on the bottom of the stack.

There was a knock at the door. I walked over to it and looked through the peephole to see Sarah standing there with her hands full. I unchained the door and let her in, grabbing my work from her hands.

"Thank you so much for coming all this way."

She looked up and saw my face, frowning. "Oh, no worries at all. I'm just glad you are okay." She leaned in for a hug as she balanced the coffee tray in her other hand.

"Yeah, kind of a crazy week."

She huffed. "I'd be lying if I didn't say that your life is a little crazy." She pointed to the table, and we walked over to coffee clutch.

"Is there a lot of talk going on at work about me?"

She shook her head. "I sent out an email after Mr. Tonic called me, stating that you were taking a few sick days. No one has questioned anything. Even Lena wanted to make sure that you had everything you needed. Can you believe that?"

We laughed. "Just keep me updated on anything that may be necessary."

She nodded as she sipped her coffee. I could see her questions rise as she studied my face.

"Was that from the man that made you cry?"

I sucked in a breath and just nodded.

"Fucking prick," she said. "I hope he got it worse."

I half smiled, "He will. They are still searching for him."

Sarah shifted in her seat, leaning closer to me, as if we were in a busy room and needed to keep things secretive. "Was it Jared?"

I met her eyes with shock. "How–"

"I recognized his voice from Lena's office and knew right away who it was. When I saw him head to the breakroom to get coffee, I switched the sugar with salt before I left the room, just for him to choke on." We both laughed at the thought.

"Thank you," I said, feeling amused at her slyness. I hoped that I never crossed her.

My phone chimed, making me jump. Sarah jumped up and grabbed it for me from across the room. "Sorry, it's Cameron, I didn't mean to peek." She smiled nervously before handing it to me. "I actually just met someone at the coffee shop with the same name."

I smiled brightly when she said it. "Lawyer, Cameron?" She stared back at me in disbelief. "687 phone number?"

"Yes." She stood, confused.

"Perfect. You better let him take you on a date."

She crossed her arms and waited for more information.

"What?" I asked.

"And here I thought that I caught the man's attention all on my own." She uncrossed her arms and sat down in the chair.

"Oh, no. I didn't tell him anything about you yet. I just knew he would be there today." I winked at her. "Please take him up on his offer."

Cameron: Two sugars with vanilla and caramel creamer and cinnamon. Why do I have this strange feeling that you are trying to send a pretty woman in place of you?

Aisling: Just go with it :)

She smiled and agreed, and after an hour of chit chatting and a tour, she decided to head back to the office.

Chapter 14
Hard Work Pays Off

I finished uploading every edit that was left on the paper manuscript and converted it into a cleaner, sleeker document to send to Marleigh to have her look at the final touches before my formatting and publishing team began. I stared at the laptop with the finished work and just smiled. I was thankful for a job that could be done from anywhere, otherwise this deadline would've been ruined. I stared for a minute longer before I decided it was perfect. The door opened before I could hit send, and Jameson walked in.

"Hey, you." His suit jacket was in hand, and his tie loosened along his neck. His tired face smiled, the now yellow bruise almost gone, thankfully. Had I not known he had it a few days ago, then it would've gone undetected. I waited as he made his way to me at the table. His eyes glanced at the screen while leaning down to kiss my cheek. "You finished," he said excitedly. "Marleigh will be happy."

I leaned up and kissed his lips. "Thank you. Hitting send in three, two, one," I said slowly, as my finger clicked the button to get it out of my hands.

"Well, that is a big accomplishment."

I covered my mouth after inhaling sharply, "Oh my god, what if she hates it all? Now I'm the one having imposter syndrome."

He laughed, "Whatever that is. You nerdy writers are so funny. She will be happy. She specifically assigned the job to you."

"Because of you."

"Nope, she has read every article that you published in the magazines before I had even mentioned that I knew you."

"You're full of shit. But I will take it." I laughed as I stood and wrapped my arms around his neck. But he seemed to be lost in deep thought. "What's happened?"

He shook his head, "Nothing that can't wait until tomorrow. Today we are celebrating." He pulled my arms from around his neck and walked to the kitchen to grab two glasses and a bottle of champagne from the wine cooler. "To your successes." He raised the glasses after being poured and smiled.

"And to yours." I raised my glass to clink his.

"Then to us." He winked and brought the bubbling liquid to his lips.

He smiled, but behind the smile something was on his mind. He wasn't going to tell me. At least, not on his own. I grabbed the champagne and poured him another glass, and another before opening a new bottle, and before I knew it, he had set down his glass and had the bottle with him as he lifted me up and threw me over his shoulder while heading to the bathroom.

He set me down gently as he walked toward the jacuzzi tub and started to run the water, adding bubbles that smelled of lavender and eucalyptus. I inhaled deeply as he walked back toward me. Not drunk, but he was finally very relaxed. The man could hold his liquor, I would give him that. As my own head started to feel a little lighter, he lifted my top over my head, then he unbuttoned his. His chest exposed as his chiseled abs flexed in front of me. He grabbed my hips and pulled me closer to him before pulling my shorts down.

"Get in," he demanded, and I obeyed, stepping out of my bottoms. Naked and exposed in front of him, both excited and nervous as my adrenaline coursed through my veins, I looked back and watched as he finished the second champagne bottle. I smirked to myself, knowing that anything I wanted to ask him would now be revealed.

I stepped into the steaming water, completely submerging myself and letting my entire body relax before coming back to the surface. Breathing in deeply, I pushed my hair out of my face. Jameson was standing next to the tub, waiting patiently for me to let him join, his naked body standing in front of me. I leaned up against the side of the tub and smiled, admiring his body in front of me, not letting him submerge yet.

"Long day?" I asked while looking up at him, letting my tits perk out from underneath me and rest on the edge of the tub. He looked down at them, his arousal apparent. I smiled and leaned back to let him join me in the bubbles.

"You always make me feel better," he whispered, as he pulled me back against his chest.

"I knew something was wrong."

He nodded. "It's just been a long day. Two more building fires started today, one at my first building I ever bought, and the second was at my first investment property, only a block away from the first. I feel like karma is kicking my ass right now." He inhaled heavily, and I could feel the weight of the destruction on him. "The cops have decided to investigate the fires, see if there's a connection with the pyro or just random teens causing shit. They believe my brother has left the city and will end the search for now to focus on the fires. That's what really pissed me off. And to top it off, the insurance companies are a bunch of assholes who are trying to get out of paying for the damages."

I turned my head to look up at him and let my brows furrow when I saw his frustration.

"That's three buildings in a week." I shook my head. "You know what, you don't need to worry about your brother. If he left, then that's even better for us both. So, that's one problem solved." He shrugged and leaned down to kiss my lips. "Your apartment is ready for you whenever you decide to go back. I set your keys next to your purse."

"Are you kicking me out already?" I asked sarcastically.

Jameson seemed to not know what sarcasm sounded like. "No, never. I prefer you to just stay here. I could make a list of reasons to stay."

I laughed and rested my head back against him and debated. "Now I want to hear that list." I mentally thought of lists, and something inside me triggered, but I couldn't place it. "But in reality, my place is closer to work."

"You can work from your laptop here."

I shook my head, brushing off the thoughts. "I eventually need to go back to my place. What are you going to do, wrap me in a bubble suit to keep me safe?"

He laughed. "That's tempting."

I playfully nudged him and laughed. "I will be fine. Besides, I don't want you to get sick of me and push me away."

When he didn't respond, I turned around in the tub to face him. He seemed lost in thought, and it made me wonder if he was going to push me away to keep me safe now. I started to panic internally. *Will he get sick of me? Have I caused too much destruction in his life already? Why does chaos follow me?* Something inside me started to get under my own skin. *Myself.*

"I didn't mean it like that. I know I have been the one to push you away for too long, and I am sorry. I just don't want to change my whole life around for someone again. I just need to keep my feet planted and keep my goals in mind too."

He smiled. "I didn't say anything."

"It was your silence that made me hear you loud and clear."

He laughed as he pushed me to the other side of the tub to face him while talking. "Where do you see yourself in five years?" he asked.

I leaned back against the edge of the tub and looked up toward the ceiling, debating on that myself. In five years, I would be thirty-seven. When I was younger, I had planned on being married, having a house, a successful career, and children by now. I laughed to myself. Real life had not turned out as I planned when I was fifteen, young and dumb.

Up until last week, I had my apartment that I could barely make rent on without a roommate. A job that was barely paying that rent, let alone groceries. Marriage hadn't even crossed my mind since I felt the betrayal of Jared years ago. And children was a tough subject, considering that I would already have a ten year old screaming at me that she knew how the world worked. I shook my head as Jameson bumped me with his leg as bringing me back to reality.

"In five years, I hope to be thriving." I exhaled slowly because it was true, only that I didn't know how I wanted to be thriving. "What about you?"

"Easy, I want to be on the moon by then, or maybe Mars," he answered confidently, and my eyes bulged at the thought. "Kidding." He laughed, then I did too. "Five years," he inhaled sharply and looked around the room. "I want to be happy. Whether that means leaving New York and living in a small town, or married with ten kids, or even being homeless and living off the land in the forest. I really don't care. I just want to be happy.

I've accomplished my career, and now I'm ready for something more, my own happiness."

"You would leave New York?"

"I will go wherever you want to go."

Butterflies fluttered inside me as I realized his five year plan had me in it. It was something I wanted to hear a decade ago, yet it felt as if no time had passed between us at this moment. I looked up at him as my cheeks blushed. Guilt began to build inside me. I could not let him ruin himself with me. He could have anyone, and he deserved someone who wouldn't fall into lies from his pathetic brother. He leaned closer toward me, gently grabbing my face.

"Best decision I ever made was going to that bar a month ago and seeing you." He kissed my lips and pulled his face away. "Please don't push me away again."

Self-doubt started to loom over me. "Ugh, you deserve someone so much better than me. I don't get why you stick around. You could have anyone. Absolutely anyone. Why me?"

"You're the only one that knows me before and after all of this. You're my Ais. It's you, it's always been you."

Fuck, I needed to hear that so much. I wanted to have it all, but then my dark, self-manipulating thoughts told me I didn't deserve him. I didn't deserve this happiness. I was a piece of shit who kept too many secrets for too long. We, as humans, accepted the love we thought we deserved, and his love for me was too much. I didn't deserve it. I didn't deserve any of this. I looked around the bathroom, as big as my whole apartment, and my stomach started to turn. It may have been the champagne, but a part of me knew that it was my own guilt of breaking his heart and him being too nice to let me back in without enough punishment. I needed to suffer longer. I needed some kind of destruction. My life could not be this perfect because of a millionaire man that was willing to let go and move on. He deserved better.

A flip switched inside of me as I stood from the tub. "Damn it, I fucked your brother only weeks after losing our baby. I don't deserve you… I'm going to leave."

Within seconds, his emotions came to the surface. I had caught him off guard. I said words that even I had not expected. My own self sabotaging mind didn't want me to be happy, even for the shortest amount of time. A decade of hating myself had finally taken its toll, and I snapped. I watched as his heart shattered in two by the venom that I didn't mean to hurt him with. I just needed him to push me away so that I didn't have to be the one to ruin him. I needed him to get rid of me like the trash that I was. And just like that, his eyes saddened. I had broken his heart, again. I truly was a piece of shit.

I stepped one foot out of the tub and quickly grabbed the towel before running out of the bathroom. I couldn't breathe. I needed oxygen, and the air inside this place was becoming too thick. I didn't deserve him or the luxury of this life. I deserved Trevor, the boyfriend that knocked me around. I deserved Jared, the man who used me and continued to blackmail me over the years. And the other countless men that belittled me and made me feel worthless. I deserved nothing as good as Jameson. I grabbed his t-shirt and shorts and my keys before running out of his suite barefoot, walking down New York's dirty sidewalks, calling a taxi to bring me home. Far away from this man who deserved better. I would only drag him down with me.

I wiped the tears away as I jumped in the first vehicle that met my wave. Not caring at this point if it was truly a taxi or not. I told him my address and watched out of the corner of my eye as Jameson reached the last stair to his place and tried to halt the cab, but we were already moving. I didn't dare turn around because I knew that his sadness would be written all over his face. The cab driver looked away from the rearview mirror and let me bawl my eyes out while ruining my very own future that could've been something special, but I just needed to save him from the heartbreak that would surely come if I stayed around.

My phone started to ring, and I looked down to see his name come across the screen. I forwarded it to voicemail as we kept driving to my place. I felt sick to my stomach, but something about a five year plan terrified me. Because a decade ago, our lives changed drastically and to think that far ahead was only torture, It would surely set me up for heartache. My mind switched back to when we were teens back in our small town.

"Promise me we will have forever."

"I promise, Ais. It will always be you." Jameson kissed me hard as we watched the sunrise along Lake Michigan. Leaning against his chest and wrapped in the fleece blanket for our monthly sunrise tradition that we started since our first official date, I grabbed his hand, knowing that he meant it.

"I love you, Jameson. I'm the luckiest girl in the world."

He kissed my head as the sun peaked along the lake, "I'm the lucky one."

The memory faded as the cab driver pulled up to my apartment. "This ride is on me, darling, please get inside safely." He nodded as he watched me wipe away the tears.

"Thank you," I said and stepped out as more tears fell. Reaching my door, I unlocked the new locking mechanism with the set of keys that Jameson had set next to my purse. I unlocked the empty apartment and just bawled, knowing that I messed up my own life again and another spiral would begin.

"Why can't I just let myself be happy? What is wrong with me? Ugh, self-sabotaging idiot," I yelled at myself before going into the bedroom where my nightmare was brought to life a week ago. I finally snapped.

"Fuck you, Jared," I screamed, as I ripped the blankets off my bed and grabbed the long mirror against the wall and tossed it hard, watching it shatter into a million pieces. I touched my face and was disgusted by the bruising that remained. "It's because of you that I hate myself. You set me up and used me. You took the one thing that was your brother's and tried to ruin it. You tried to ruin me." The tears flowed uncontrollably now as I tiptoed around the broken glass and tried to escape my room, escape my apartment, escape my life. I just couldn't make a list of a bullshit five year plan that I couldn't promise. A stupid fucking list that meant absolutely nothing but broken promises. A list that would surely burn itself from the lies.

A burning list.

A list that burns.

A list.

A thought came to me as the word struck a nerve.

The cops couldn't find Jared, but I knew exactly where he would be next if he was still in New York. It had to be him causing the chaos and starting the fires. Why wouldn't it be him? Wherever there were problems, it was because of Jared. He's setting those fires to lure me out to him. And this time, I knew exactly where he would strike next. He was going in order of Jameson's successful purchases. Each time Jameson bought a large building, Jared would text me and keep them in order, each new place added to the list. He was jealous to the extreme, and that was his jealousy list, with my name at the top now crossed off. He wouldn't let me have happiness while he still felt abandoned.

I grabbed a change of clothes and walked into the bathroom, rushing cold water over my face and securing my still damp hair in a bun on top of my head. I turned to head out the door and confront him myself.

But I froze as I looked at my bruised self in front of the mirror and realized that I couldn't take him on alone.

"What am I doing? This isn't me," I whispered to myself.

I grabbed my phone and dialed the police.

"Anonymous tip, the pyro is going to strike at Mr. Tonic's real estate office next." I hung up the phone and sat back on the edge of the tub.

"Please catch him," I whispered while bringing my phone to my forehead and trying to slow my breathing.

Ten minutes later, my phone rang again with a blocked caller.

"Hello?"

"Ma'am, thank you for the tip, but unfortunately, we were too late. It had already happened. If you have another one, please inform us. Thank you for trying."

At least my theory was right. He was going down the list, meaning he had three more big places to burn before he went after my publishing company and destroy yet another piece of my life.

Pounding on the door made me jump out of my skin. I ran to the hallway with my voice shaking, "Who is it?"

"Ais, it's me," Jameson's voice yelled through the door. "Open the door."

I stepped toward the door and froze. If I let him in here, then he would try and convince me that I was good, that I deserved happiness. I didn't want to hear any of those lies right now. His own brother was burning his places down because of me. It was me. I was part of the chaos too.

"Hello? Yes, this is him. Are you fucking kidding me?" Jameson's voice boomed in the apartment hall. I walked forward to peek at who he was talking to. He stood in sweatpants and a white tee with his phone to his ear, shaking his head. "Yes, I'll be right there. Thank you." He hung up the phone and punched the wall, then paced back and forth. "Ais, I'm coming back for you. I'm sorry if I triggered something. I didn't mean to hurt you."

I laid my head against the door and sank to the floor. Again, he was taking all the blame. Always the better person.

"There's been another fire. Please stay here," he said through the door, and I could almost feel him leaning against me through the door. I wanted so badly to be next to him and go with him to help take the weight off his shoulders, but in the long run, I would be the weight to drag him down. To keep him safe, I needed to let him go.

Chapter 15
He's Never Going to Stop

I crawled onto the couch, grabbed the blanket off the chair, and decided to have a lonely night. Then, come tomorrow, I would wake up and conquer the world. Well, my publishing world anyway. And I decided that tomorrow I was going to do exactly what I shouldn't. I was going after Jared once and for all.

The morning came fast, my phone was silent and my apartment was empty. The loud thunder made me sit up quickly and head to the window. New York was drowning in long overdue rain. Would Jared dare to start a fire during a storm? It would be pointless and unsuccessful, which meant I had a few more hours to decide on my own plan. The only way he was going to stop was if he had me, and that was not something that was going to happen.

I walked to the kitchen and made a pot of coffee. My hands were shaking as I tried to pour my mug full, spilling half the coffee onto the counter, and seeping into the drawer under it. I opened the top drawer to quickly clean up the spill and froze as I pulled out the handgun that Trevor had left behind like the idiot that he was. He took me shooting at the range for our first date, which should've been my first red flag, but in actuality, I was glad to have learned how to use it. I checked the cartridge and noticed that it was full. I emptied it, dropping the bullets into the top drawer. It would be nice to keep it with me, but I would never be able to kill anyone with it. I just wanted to scare him. I didn't actually want to use it on him. I just needed him to be scared enough to never come back here and try to ruin me or his brother again. Having him far away could finally let me forgive myself with the secret finally being out.

I slipped on my high waisted pants with a blouse that had my cleavage scream, "buy me a drink." I grabbed my flats as my phone rang. I ran out to the living room and answered without looking at the name.

"Hello?"

"Hey, it's me, well, Marleigh." She laughed. "You're not going to believe this, but I received the edits last night and agree with every single one. I loved the way you reworded multiple sentences and had zero complaints. So, I did something."

My heart froze as I waited for her next words.

"I hope you wanted 'Aisling Lux, Mark My Words Publishing' on the copyright page. I made sure they had your name stand out as both the editor and owner of the company. It's being sent off for printing at the end of the day. I couldn't wait."

Speechless, I processed what she was saying.

"Aisling, are you listening? Your company will be number one in New York by the end of next week with this book."

"Oh my god. I... I am speechless. I am so excited. Wow."

"I know, right? Now, Monday can be launch day."

"Marleigh, congratulations, I am so happy that we worked out for you."

She laughed, "Are you kidding me? You and your company will have every book of mine from here on out. You just landed New York's bestselling author's lifetime business."

"Eeeeek," I squealed, as did she. "Please tell me you are jumping up and down like I am."

We both laughed. "Congratulations, Miss Aisling Lux. This is very well deserved for you. Your work is exquisite, and I wish you would've been around for my first ten books. Love you, lady. Proud of you." The line disconnected as I sat down on the couch in awe and just soaked in an achievement that I had been working on for so long. I wonder what Devon's face would look like when he realized what he just signed over to Jameson.

Jameson.

My thoughts wandered to his whereabouts, and without thinking, I dialed his number.

"Are you okay?" he answered.

I froze as I remembered how I left him. "Oh, I, um–"

"Ais, hold on. Marleigh is calling me."

I hung up, not knowing what more to say. I was so excited, and he was dealing with his brother, the pyro. It was as if the universe would not let him and me be happy at the same time. I put on enough concealer to hide my wounds and grabbed my purse, jacket, umbrella, and the unloaded gun before walking out the door. Marleigh would fill him in on my excitement, and he would understand why I called.

Reaching the bottom stair of my apartment, I opened my umbrella as I waved for a taxi.

"Uptown please. The Luxy Hotel and Suites please."

"Yes, ma'am." The driver nodded and headed for the next building that would be targeted.

Aisling: I'm sorry about last night. I have a theory about your pyro.
Jameson: Where are you?
Aisling: Testing my theory.
Jameson: Don't do anything stupid.

The chimes stopped as the ringer began. I forwarded his calls to voicemail as we drove to the hotel. I just needed to see if Jared was there. I would keep my distance, but I needed to catch him at the place of the chaos to bring it to Jameson and the police. They both had enough on their plates. And I could be wrong.

I paid the driver and walked into the hotel that was taller than the rest in the city. The chandeliers brilliantly shined in the lobby. I walked past the beautiful entryway and walked straight to the bar. Watching as lonely men stared. I shook the rain off me and laid my jacket carefully behind my tall chair. I waited a brief moment to scan the room while the bartender asked what I was having. When I ordered a Brandy Old Fashioned Sweet, he smiled and nodded, going to mix the concoction.

I turned and scanned the bar, only to feel disappointed and relieved that Jared was not where I suspected him to be. The bartender came back with my drink, tipping him. I reached for my phone and pulled up a photo of Jared.

"Hey, excuse me. Have you seen this man here today?"

The bartender squinted, "Please tell me you are not on a date with the owner's brother."

I laughed. "So, you do know him. Has he been here today?"

He exhaled smoothly. "I saw him earlier with another blonde, please don't waste your time with him. You seem like a good gal."

I smirked. "Trust me, I'm not." I sipped the drink and let it go down smooth. He knew how to make it to perfection. Of course he would. Jameson only hired the best. I rolled my eyes and turned my chair to face the entryway to wait for the pyro.

A half hour passed when I watched as Jameson walked through the front door and headed straight to the bar by me. My jaw dropped as he made eye contact with me.

The bartender whispered from behind me, "Sorry, darling. I can't let his brother ruin you too. Too many women have cried in your exact chair because of him."

I jumped at his voice. If only he already knew the tears I've cried because of him.

Jameson reached me and sat in the open chair next to me, nodding at the bartender before he turned my chair to face him. His hand touched my thigh as his gaze locked with mine.

"Do not ignore me."

I swallowed hard. "I wasn't ignor–"

"Stop thinking that you deserve to be treated like shit. You are not bad, not by any means." He leaned in closer as he whispered, "Maybe in the sheets." He winked as he pulled back away from me, waving for a drink for himself.

The bartender walked over with a matching Old Fashioned and smiled at the both of us before going back to shining the glasses, smirking.

"This was your theory? Letting your cleavage hang out for every man to drool over while you pushed me further away?"

I looked down and gently tugged at my shirt, embarrassed now. "Not intentionally. I, well, I think the pyro is…" I froze, not wanting to involve him further. If I could just… I had no idea what I was doing. Maybe I really did have a concussion from last week. "I think it's Jared."

His eyes bulged as he huffed. "He wouldn't burn my buildings."

I nodded, "I think he would, and I think he has."

He straightened his suit and leaned back in the chair. "Why are you looking for him alone?"

"I wanted to get proof and make sure my judgment wasn't clouded by hate."

"If, and I mean if, it is him, then why are you at The Luxy?"

I grabbed my phone and searched Jared's old conversation and handed him my phone. "Jared, use to send me a list of your accomplishments. Buildings, screenshots of magazines, names of women. Everything that you accomplished in the exact order of when it happened."

"The women are a lie, but the buildings are right." He scanned the lists again before looking up in shock. "The Luxy," his eyes met mine with concern. "This place is next on the list. I'm going to kill him myself then."

I shook my head, "That is exactly why I didn't involve you. I wanted to get proof for the police so they could arrest him if I was right."

"Fuck that. He's mine to ruin now."

"Jameson, you can't do anything. That's exactly what he wants. He wants paparazzi to catch you ruining your reputation. You really think a brawl in the middle of New York is going to look good for you?"

He grabbed his drink and lifted it up, taking it as if it were a shot. "Another," he waved to the bartender, frustrated. "Fine, I'll call the police."

The bartender looked up with concern, "Sir, I'm afraid that won't be necessary." He nodded his head toward the entry as a group of policemen stormed into the building, wearing protective gear.

"Everyone out, there has been a bomb threat," the man yelled, as he pulled the fire alarm. Chaos started as men and women screamed and ran out of the building. Jameson looked back at me, as we stayed seated. Shock reached both of us, and at the same time, we both said the next building on the list, "The pub."

He grabbed my hand as he led us both out of the hotel, knowing damn well that there was no bomb if it was Jared's doing, but it could very well be a distraction while he hit the next building on his list only five blocks away.

"Get in," he demanded, and we drove in silence.

We were too late. The pub had been evacuated, and the street was being blocked by citizens watching the blaze of the entire building. Anger filled Jameson's face as he walked closer to the flames. "Is everyone out? Everyone is safe?" he yelled at the manager, who was in shock but nodded.

I pulled on his arm, bringing him further away from the heat and trying to keep him out of harm's way. That only meant that one other building was left before my publishing company would be burned to the ground.

I dialed the police and waited for the answer. "Tonic Stocks and Mark My Words are next on the list for the pyro–"

Jameson grabbed the phone, "This is Jameson Tonic. I need squads outside of those buildings now.

The pyro is Jared Tonic. Yes, ma'am. Thank you." He handed the phone back to me and ushered me back to his car, opening the door and securing me inside. "Damn it. I didn't want to believe it. It's fucking him. What a piece of shit. He's worse than our father was. Jealousy has consumed him."

I sat back and watched as the flames burned the building down. "What now?"

He contemplated our next move before turning toward me. "You are going back home while I take care of this."

"Excuse you?"

"I cannot let you get in the middle of this."

I laughed out of my own anger, "I am the reason for all of this."

"Just give me a weekend. I'll fly you to Wisconsin for the weekend. You can be back by Monday. If everything burns, then at least I will know that you were nowhere near the flames"

"You're coming with me." I wasn't giving him the option. If I left him here alone, then he would surely hunt down his own brother and kill him, and that would haunt him for life.

His face looked tired, and he didn't dare try to fight with me on this. "Okay."

"Okay. Official book launch is Monday. I need to be back by then, whether the company is standing or not. Deal?"

He nodded as he laid his head back against the headrest and watched the firefighters extinguish the block's favorite bar. I watched him, as a decade of his accomplishments were destroyed from underneath him by his own blood. I grabbed his hand and decided that I needed to make him smile again. Because tonight I was going to let love win, through all of this chaos.

"Can I take you out for dinner, my treat?" I asked.

He laughed, "I can take you out."

"No, it's my treat. Let's just forget the world for a night and be back in Wisconsin by tomorrow. One week," I lifted my finger sternly, "and this will all be over."

He nodded as he put his car in reverse and drove back to the busy city.

"Where are we forgetting the world tonight?"

I smiled. "Turn right at the next set of lights."

He obliged, as we made our way to a mini grocery store just outside of my apartment. Confused, he pulled over to park.

"I'll be right back," I said, as I hopped out of the car.

Running inside to grab peanut butter, jelly, bread, and pickles. I ran down the next aisle, grabbing the premixed Brandy Old Fashioned and cherries. Then, I quickly grabbed his favorite bag of chocolates and plastic utensils before paying and running back to the car with my paper bags.

"Okay, please drive us to Homerun Haven."

"All of that just to go to the bar?" he laughed, confused.

"Just drive," I demanded.

He parked, lucky to have gotten a close parking spot as we walked into the building. I smiled and waved to

Sarah working behind the bar. I pointed to the roof and she nodded.

"It's all yours." She smiled and handed me the key and two empty glasses.

"Come on."

"Isn't that your assistant?" he asked, confused.

"Yes, her parents own this bar. She helps out every Sunday night so they can have their date night. It's tradition, so I let her start late every Monday and pay her the same rate for a full day." I smiled as I grabbed his hand and dragged him upstairs, unlocking the rooftop and switching the lights on before entering.

The lights twinkled against the forming night's sky, and the city lights surrounding us made for a night to remember. The ground was still wet from the earlier rain, but the patio table and chairs could be wiped off. I moved the chairs closer together, facing out toward the city, and set up our dinner date. Jameson watched intently as I pulled the pickles out and laid them across the peanut butter slab of bread and then the jelly.

"Are you kidding me? You still eat those?" he laughed.

"You mean, *we* still eat these? You think life is all about fine dining and personal trainers? This is our roots. This is simple. This is us." I slammed the two halves together and handed one to him. "Sit."

He smirked before grabbing the sandwich and sitting in the wet chair, not bothering to wipe it off. I laughed as I made another one and joined him in the wet seat, lifting the sandwich to him, "Cheers to everything fucked and everything good all at once."

He snorted. "You can say that again." We clinked sandwiches as I poured us each a glass.

I looked at his watch and smiled. "Just wait, my favorite part is coming."

"Oh yeah?" he questioned, waiting for an explanation. But when I stayed silent, he decided to fill the quiet. "Are you done running from me?"

I inhaled slowly, knowing this question was coming and I really wanted to avoid it. I rolled my eyes and stared out at the billboard in the distance waiting for it to change.

"Ais, come on. You deserve happiness too."

"Haven't you noticed that only one of us can have it at a time? We are cursed. Our whole life has been a twist of meetings, always turning into chaos."

"That's not true. If I never would have left–"

"You needed to leave. All of this," I lifted my arms and pointed to half of New York, "is because you are a genius and invested in businesses as a leap of faith, and your name is known to the world now because of it."

He shook his head. "My world is quite lonely behind my work. What kind of life is that?"

"So, get a wife or a puppy." I smirked. "Someone who deserves your goodness."

He stood and set down his sandwich before walking over to me, laying out his hand in front of me, waiting for me to take it. I inhaled slowly and exhaled. "How can I show you that you deserve the world, this world, any world? You deserve happiness more than anyone."

When I didn't grab his hand, he lifted me out of the chair and over his shoulder, making me squirm and giggle. I let my self-doubt disappear for a second. He spanked my ass while he turned me around in circles. "You're so bad." He spanked me again and laughed.

"Hey," I laughed. "Put me down. Jameson. Put. Me. Down." I kicked in the air playfully as he set me down. Dizziness kicked in as I grabbed his watch. "Okay, wait." I stepped back from his playfulness and made him turn toward the city lights. "Just look in three, two, one." I counted down with my fingers as I pointed toward the billboard. Jameson watched as he smiled and laughed.

"Really, Ais?"

I watched him blush with embarrassment as his face showed up on the billboard, exactly the same time every night.

"It's my favorite view of the city at this exact time." I moved my arms around, jokingly pretending to have not noticed the ginormous billboard with his face on it. "Oh, you thought it was you?" I laughed and poked at him before wrapping my arms around his neck and leaning up to kiss him. "Kidding, it is you."

He lifted me up and wrapped my legs around his back, kissing my lips before moving to my neck, then to my chest. I tilted my face up to the night sky, forgetting about all the bullshit for a second and just enjoying his presence.

"Please forgive me?" I asked without looking away from the sky.

"There's nothing to be forgiven," He said between kisses on my body.

"I think I just need to hear it."

He snorted. "Well, if that's all it took for you to stop pushing me away, then you're forgiven a thousand times over." He pulled me closer into his chest and hugged me tight.

I felt tears start to form in the corners of my eyes as the weight of the world lifted by hearing those words. Something I needed to hear for more than a decade. A secret regret that needed to be released long ago. A moment that I had never thought I would have, but very much needed. I smiled as I wiped the tears away, feeling free for the first time in a long time from my own hate.

The night sky started to rain, then turned into a downpour as he held me against his chest. I grabbed his face and pulled it up to mine and kissed him with all my regrets surfacing and letting the cold rain wash away our past and give us a fresh start. And in this moment, I felt happy. Didn't matter how much had happened over the last few weeks, this moment right here was the happiness I needed to feel to set myself free.

We laughed as he set me down but held me closer to him, not letting the weather ruin our date.

"It will pass," he said.

Unsure if he was talking about the weather or something else entirely, I decided not to overthink it and just enjoy the night.

"So, is this our first official date?"

I laughed. "I think we're long past our first date."

"Good." He grabbed my face and let his lips crush back into mine. His tongue played twister with mine as I felt the sadness inside me slowly dissolve.

Chapter 16
Home Sweet Home

The airport wasn't busy at all. It seemed as if not many people wanted to travel to the farmlands of Wisconsin, and yet here we were, making a last minute getaway together back home. I looked over and saw Jameson's nerves come to light as his leg continued to bounce while waiting at the airport. I laid my hand on his thigh, hoping to steady him.

"When was the last time you were home?"

He inhaled sharply. "Well, probably about six years ago."

My eyes widened as I realized the timeframe.

"But that was–"

"Yes, I know. It's been six years, and I can't seem to make my way back there ever since. As shitty of a house we lived in, my mother was the only one that made the house a home." He looked up, eyes sad.

"Well, let's bring her flowers, I'm sure she would love that very much."

He nodded as our tickets were called to be seated. I wrapped my arm under his as we walked onto the flight to head back home, where it all began.

The flight was short, by the time the attendants reached our aisle for a drink order, the pilot had already announced we would be landing soon, ahead of schedule. I had mixed feelings about being back home. Wisconsin was my everything growing up, and I never thought that I would want to leave it. Up until my world spiraled anyway, then I needed a change of scenery and to forget about all the reminders of my past.

"Do your parents know about…" he pointed to my abdomen and waited.

I nodded, "Yes, my mom was very supportive during it. It was her idea to get a fresh start away from here."

He exhaled slowly, seeming relieved in knowing that I wasn't fully alone in a secret that I kept from him. "Let's head to your family first. You know my dad is probably at the bar right now anyways."

"It's ten in the morning." I stopped walking in disbelief.

Jameson laughed, "You know his body's fuel is alcohol. Breakfast, lunch, and dinner. He's been begging to leave this world since my mom died." He shrugged and continued to walk to the luggage pickup, grabbing both suitcases and refusing to let me help.

After an hour of driving, we pulled into my parents' driveway. I could see my parents sitting in their recliners and watching television. My mom must've seen the headlights as we pulled in because she jumped up and stared out of the bay window before squealing with excitement as she rushed toward the door.

"Well, here goes nothing," I said, as I stepped out of the car and walked toward the door. My mom ran outside and hugged me hard. I hadn't known that I needed such an embrace until she squeezed me tight. The weight of the world disappeared, and I was home.

"Hi, Mom." I smiled and waited until she loosened her grip.

"You didn't tell me you were coming," she turned and yelled back into the house. "Honey, turn the oven on, our baby is home." She giggled like a child before looking past me and realizing I had brought company. She gasped. "Does he know?"

I nodded, smiling. Knowing the weight had finally been lifted after a decade.

"Good," she kissed my forehead before walking past me and pulling Jameson in for a long overdue hug. "Welcome home, honey."

"Thank you, Mrs. Lux. It's so nice to see you."

"Oh, you," she blushed. "You better be taking care of my daughter."

"Yes, ma'am." He looked up and smirked at me.

"Let's get you inside and get some lunch made," she said while rubbing his shoulder and leading him in the house.

I stood outside and stared at the house, remembering the many good memories that this home gave me and smiling to myself, happy to be home and have Jameson with me. For the first time in a long time, the world felt right, and even though we have a lot of drama going on back in New York, here the world seemed calm and peaceful.

"Hey, kiddo. You coming in to join us?" my dad spoke, as he stepped onto the front porch, smiling.

I met his smile and walked up, kissing him on the cheek. "It's good seeing you, Dad."

"Likewise."

The house was exactly as I remembered it. We sat around the kitchen table, sharing stories of mostly Jameson and his successes. My parents had been mostly up to date with my life over the years through phone calls, but to have Jameson conversations again, my dad was happy.

"You're the first guy she's brought back home with her, ever." My dad laughed as he elbowed Jameson's shoulder.

"Oh, really?" Jameson asked. "You sure you're not just saying that to make me feel less intimidated?"

We all laughed as my dad shook his head.

"How long are you planning on staying?" my mom asked.

"Well, I think we are just staying the weekend–"

"Yes, Ais has a huge book deal on Monday that we need to be back for. She is now the owner of Mark My Words and signed a huge deal with Marleigh."

"Miss Aisling, you did not tell us that!" my mother exclaimed. "Marleigh? As in, Marleigh Englewood? The author?"

I nodded.

Her jaw dropped as she stood up from the table and walked back in with a stack of books. "Could you maybe have her sign these for me?"

I laughed and grabbed the stack of books. "Only if you come visit me in New York this year for the holidays."

"Deal."

"Then we can even arrange a meet and greet," Jameson chimed in. "She's a friend of ours."

My mom's excitement was beyond anything I had seen. I thought her happiness to see me was going to be enough, but to meet the author of her favorite books was even more so.

"Do you guys have a hotel?" my dad asked.

"Yes, we're booked up the road at the inn."

"You sure you don't want to stay here?"

I shook my head, "I think my twin bed may be a little small for me now." I laughed as Jameson grabbed my hand on top of the table and rubbed it gently, making me stop in this moment and appreciate the PDA. My mom caught my stare and met my eyes with a gentle smile. She nodded and seemed happy for me. Hours passed, before I knew it the sun was starting to go down as we reminisced.

"Well, I think it's time we made our way to check in. Plus, I have to stop by my dad's house and make sure he's still breathing." Jameson laughed, but behind his composure, I could sense his nervousness coming to the surface.

I stood up to move my parents' attention on me instead. "Good idea."

"Why don't you two fly back with us on Monday and come and meet Marleigh? I can have a room ready for you both." He suggested.

I glanced at him, ready to shake my head, to keep them out of danger.

"It would be nice for Ais to have some company at the book launch."

Then, I realized what he was doing. He wasn't putting them in danger, but instead keeping extra eyes on me to keep me safe. I nodded and smiled.

"We would love to," my dad announced without even talking to his better half.

"Great, I will call the airlines and get two seats added on for departure."

My dad nodded before walking over to me and hugging me tight. "Looks like we will be seeing you soon." He smiled and shook Jameson's hand before walking out of the kitchen.

My mom made her way to me and kissed my cheek, "Thank you for coming home." She then walked to Jameson and pulled him in tight for a hug. "I'm sorry for your loss. I truly hope that you and Ais can have a brighter future together," she whispered, meaning the words to be for only him, but her hearing must be weakening. I laughed to myself and smiled at the unexpected but much needed reunion.

"Okay, Mom. You have to let him go now." I laughed.

She released him and chuckled while wiping a tear from her cheek. "It's just nice seeing you two together and smiling. That's all."

"Agreed," Jameson said, as the gentleman that he is, kissing her other cheek.

Before leaving, I opened my suitcase and transferred the gun back into my purse, for my own personal safety. My security had been messed with over the past weeks, and the little piece of metal made me feel a little better. Especially knowing that we had to go to the house where my trust became broken. I made a mental note to buy some pepper spray when I get back to New York. We pulled up to his childhood home and noticed not a single light was left on. Jameson made a low growl that was meant for his ears only before exhaling slowly. "Damn it, he's still at the bar."

"Are you sure? Maybe he's–"

He pointed at the door before rolling his eyes.

"Oh, he still leaves the door cracked when he's at the bar." I laughed quietly. "Hard to believe he still trusts this small town to not break-in."

He laughed. "He never remembers his keys, let alone how to unlock the door with liquor in his veins."

Chapter 17
This Ends Now

Waiting in his old home brought back many memories. Some that I was rather not fond of, but a lot of my teen years were spent right here with Jameson by my side. I knew that the car ride back home with his dad was not going to be pleasant, so I decided to wait here and sip on the honey tea that his mother had always kept stocked in the house for everyone. At least his dad kept that tradition up. I walked around the house, turning the lights on in each room, trying to brighten the place up a little more than it had been in years.

I couldn't believe it had been six years since his mom had passed away. His probents were not great parents together, but she sure did try to do her best with the little they had. I walked to the hallway and froze outside of Jameson's old bedroom, knowing damn well that the last time I was here I had made a mistake that I now had to live with. My insides tightened, and I felt sick for a brief moment before reminding myself that the secret was out, and it was no longer just my burden.

Inching my way closer to his door, I placed my hand on the handle and sucked in a breath of air, hoping that when I opened it that demons didn't fly out at me and drag me to hell for the trouble I caused.

Damn it.

I had to stop cutting myself down. Today was a fresh start.

I grabbed the handle and pushed the door open.

Standing there feeling foolish, I realized the room had become storage over the years. His room was still the same, but extra boxes were strewn throughout the room now.

I exhaled slowly as I pushed the boxes out of the way and made my way to his old bed. Sitting on the navy blue comforter and dusting the surface with my hand, I stared at the walls filled with his highschool diploma, college acceptance letter, baseball team photo and a picture of him and his mom at Lake Michigan as a kid. I smiled at the peaceful and happy memories, closing my eyes and trying to remember only the good.

"Well, this brings back memories."

I jumped as his voice brought shivers up my spine. I looked up and saw Jared standing in the doorway watching me intently. His face was furious, and I could smell the liquor on him from across the room. He shook the bottle of whiskey and smirked as he took a step toward me.

"Get back," I warned him.

He spat on the floor. "You fucking bitch. You told him everything." His words slurred as he pulled a letter from his pocket and unraveled it while taking another step toward me.

I grabbed the letter with shaking hands and quickly scanned it over. It was Jameson's letter to me. Words swam in my vision, *baby, Jared, forgiven*. My entire body shook with nerves, and adrenaline started to course through my veins as my fight or flight mode kicked in. He had me alone in here. He was drunk. He was furious that he had lost, and his world was collapsing even further as the cops were closing in on him. I needed to get out of here and fast.

"Just stop, Jared. What are you doing here?" I steadied myself on the edge of the bed as I tried to keep my voice from quivering.

He snorted as he tipped his head back, taking another swig. "Where else was I supposed to go? You took everything from me."

"Me? Jared, you're drunk–"

"Stop trying to turn this around on me, you told Lena to leave me, you told my brother of our love–"

"It wasn't love," I snapped back. "You tried to blackmail him and me–"

Jared flew across the room and pushed me back against the bed while his whiskey filled breath lingered in my ear. I held my breath, trying to keep myself calm. Maybe if I stayed still long enough, then he would pass out and forget I was even here. I could feel the tears starting as I tried to not relive the last time we were here in this exact spot.

"Stop pretending that we didn't have something special. Years of you being around and always making time for me, and you never had feelings for me?" he slurred.

"Of course I cared for you, Jared. We grew up together. We were friends. But I loved Jameson. I love him, it's always been Jameson."

He stood and wiped his lower lip as he steadied himself.

"Jared, let's get you to your room. I think you need sleep." I offered, as I found the courage to stand and reach for his arm, trying to contain my own trembling.

"Sleep isn't going to cure me. The cops are looking for me. The girl that I fucked left me, and now the woman that I love doesn't love me back. What is sleep going to do for me?" he pushed me away from him. "All I ever wanted was to take what was mine. But instead, my brother got everything."

I stayed silent and let him ramble. Then, the energy in the room shifted, and I looked up at him as his face became furious.

"You're not listening," he accused me. Only, my mind was still in shock that he wasn't in New York being arrested by now. I needed to get to my phone in my purse. I took one more step trying to pull him with me. But before I could do anything, I felt his fist come down on my cheekbone, and my body shifted at the unexpected blow. Then, another fist reached my skull as I fell to the floor. I watched him drop over my body, and I felt his hands come across my throat as he began to strangle me. Shock and adrenaline coursed through me. I couldn't feel a damn thing. I took my fist and swung it hard toward him and kneed him in his dick, praying it'd get him off me. He loosened his grip as I gasped for air, trying to get off the ground.

"You bitch," he yelled, as he hit me again, only this time I was able to block it and pushed him back and off me. Wiping my bottom lip as the cut reopened from the other week, I ran for the kitchen where my purse laid open on the table, using the wall for support. I rummaged through it and tried to get my phone, but instead, my fingers touched the cold metal piece that had been with me since the last fiasco. My gun was in my palm, and without thinking, I grabbed it. I pulled it out, pointing it back toward the hallway as my other hand searched for my phone. My body was shaking while I debated on running, but I knew that the next house was a mile down the road, and by the time I got anywhere, Jared would catch up with me.

His body reached the hallway as he stumbled out toward me, freezing when he saw the gun pointed toward him. He laughed with annoyance.

"Fucking do it. Pull the trigger. I know it's what you've wanted for a decade. You wished the secret was gone along with me."

My hands shook. He wasn't wrong, but I was no killer nor did I want him dead. I just wanted him less heartless and to love his brother more. I wished he wasn't so manipulative.

"Jared," my voice shook. "Please, just stay back." Tears started to spill over as I tried to keep my emotions reeled in, but my head was throbbing, and I wanted to vomit.

He growled, as he took another step. "Why can't you just love me? Why can't anyone love me?" his voice shook as tears welled in his eyes. I watched as his eyes met mine, and he realized what he had just done. His expression changed to fear as he saw my face bleeding.

"Ais, I'm so sor–" he struggled with the apology, foreign words on his tongue.

I could see headlights approaching as he continued to stumble over his words. I prayed that it was and wasn't Jameson at the same time, because the thought of seeing this encounter was not going to be good.

"You're really going to shoot me?" he asked, as he took another step toward me, testing me.

"Jared, stop. Please. I don't want to do this," I screamed.

He wiped his tears, and his emotions were that of a drunk, unstable. He was hopeless to try and reason with. There was no talking to him. The door opened as Jameson walked in with his dad slung across his shoulder, another drunk in the house. Now this was a normal Tonic family reunion that I remembered, the only thing missing was their mother crying in the kitchen. So much dysfunction, and now I completely regretted coming back here.

Jameson's eyes met mine with horror as he stepped into a situation that should have never been. He quickly set his father down on the bench next to the door, but before I turned my eyes back around, I felt the gun being pulled from my hands, my head being hit by the back handle, making the room become blurry as my knees hit the ground. My hand automatically went to the back of my head and returned with blood dripping from my fingertips as I tried to rub the pain away.

Jameson didn't miss a beat. He jumped across the room and tackled Jared to the floor as he continued to beat his head into the ground. Jared got his fist around Jameson's torso and went for his kidneys, making Jameson groan out in pain and giving Jared the moment he needed to get out from underneath him. Turning around and lifting me off my feet, he brought the gun to my head, screaming.

"One fucking move and I'll kill her," Jared yelled.

Jameson stood with his hands in surrender, "Jared, let her go. This is between you and me."

"It's not," he laughed. "Ais was mine before you came back. You had the career, and I had her. You can't have it all."

"Brother, you're drunk."

Everything was happening so fast that I couldn't process anything.

"Why should you get to have it all?" Jared screamed. "I am tired… I am tired of being the black sheep."

"So don't be," I whispered. "Let me go."

He shifted his body to hold me tighter as he aimed the gun at Jameson.

"There is no letting go. My life is over, and I'm taking you with me, brother," he said, as he pulled the trigger that was pointing toward Jameson's heart. My entire body froze as I watched the gun click over and then clicked again.

Empty.

I smiled as I watched Jameson process the unloaded gun that in other circumstances would've ended his life. He jumped up and pushed the gun out of Jared's hand and threw him back against the wall.

"You tried to kill me?" he screamed in Jared's face. "Your own brother? What the fuck is wrong with you? You hate me that much?"

Jared spat as fear crossed his face. I stood motionless behind them, watching the long overdue encounter and trying to process the fact that Jared had really been out for blood. I jumped when I saw the red and blue lights flashing across the yard as they reached the driveway.

I turned around to see their dad leaning against the wall still sitting on the mudroom bench with his phone in hand. I watched him carefully as he wiped a tear from his cheek. "I failed him," he whispered to himself. I realized he saw the whole thing, even behind drunken eyes. I hoped that tonight would be a wake up call to him too at how broken his family was and he was no help to any of them.

The police rushed into the home and detained Jameson and cuffed Jared. Both were bloodied and bruised, both physically and mentally.

"He has a warrant for his arrest," Jameson exclaimed to the officers, as they walked him past me.

"I'm sorry, Aisling," Jared said.

My stomach turned at the words that should've been said years ago after he used and manipulated me. Words that I had hoped to one day be able to tell myself. I gasped as he walked past me and out the door. Now out of my life. For good, I hoped.

I stood speechless in our small town in Wisconsin where it all began and ended, and relief finally washed over me. I jumped when a hand reached for my shoulders, turning me around. Jameson froze and waited for me to process everything before lifting me into his arms.

Tears flowed as I realized we were free. The fires would stop, the blackmailing would end, and the self-sabotage could finally begin to heal. He pushed my hair out of my face and pulled me tighter against him. "Let's get out of here," he whispered, as he carried me outside of the pile of wood that would never be a home.

The night was rough after being checked out at the hospital, then the rest of the night was spent tossing and turning while we both laid in bed at the hotel. Neither of us wanted this weekend to be what it turned out to be, but then again, we were both happy that the building fires would finally stop. His insurance companies would be able to sleep better tonight too.

"Can we go somewhere?" he whispered to me.

I perked up and nodded. "Please."

We dressed warm in layers of sweatpants and jackets before heading to the car. We drove silently in the early morning. The sky was still dark but would eventually start to become lighter, I hoped as I thought of our night and hoped the same would be true for his family's healing. We reached the rocks along the shore of Lake Michigan and parked the car, climbing our way across the boulders to our old spot. I laughed as we both had muscle memory of where we were going without saying a word.

"The sun will be up soon," I said softly. While trying not to wake the world just yet, we sat and leaned against each other, letting our shoulders become slightly lighter of our troubles and balance each other out.

He snorted. "After everything tonight, I have to admit I'm happy to see another sunrise." He pulled me tighter against him and exhaled slowly.

I tried to push the night's events out of my mind and just focused on his closeness. "Jameson, I'm so sor–"

"You really need to stop apologizing for things out of your control." He sighed and kissed my forehead. "Ais, please let it go. I love you today as much as I loved you years ago. I'm not going anywhere, and you need to know that. I mean, if you'll let me stay."

I shifted to grab his letter out of my pocket and read it fully. He watched me, confused as to what I was doing, but then smirked and nodded while he stayed silent.

Ais,

My world is nothing without you in it. Everything with Jared can be forgiven as long as you forgive yourself first. I am sorry that he hurt you because of me. I hope that we can have the future that WE deserve together and can get past this. Anything that involves you will help with my happiness journey, and I hope with yours too. So, whenever you are ready to start fresh with me, just tell me to STAY.

I love you, Ais, with all my heart.
-Jameson
P.S. We can keep practicing on making a baby until we are ready to have one again.

I felt the tears forming at the sweet promise, and I needed to say something to break it. "You should probably leave." I laughed as he did. "But I would prefer it if you stayed." I turned and quickly looked up at him, studying his beautiful features and feeling every bit of him becoming brighter and hoping that the future between us would last a lifetime. I picked up his hand and held it out in front of me, his fingers interlocking between mine. I kissed his hand and held it closer to my body and hoped that he would never let me go. I wanted him with me now and always, and I was finally going to let myself have the happiness that I had been pushing away for far too long. His lips reached mine, kissing me back slowly and sweet.

"I can do that," he whispered.

"Forever?"

"And ever."

ABOUT THE AUTHOR

After publishing multiple novels under a pen name, Avery Queen has been enjoying her journey in the adult romance world. With her next novella 'You Should Probably Leave,' she's giving readers a taste of what is to come. She plans to continue to write while living with her husband and dog. She's found passion in more than just the pages she writes, including hiking, kayaking, and traveling. She's happy to be following her dream as a full-time writer.